BEST GAY
ROMANCE
2010

BEST GAY
ROMANCE
2010

Edited by
Richard Labonté

CLEIS
PRESS

Published in the United States.
Cleis Press Inc., P.O. Box 14697, San Francisco, California 94114.

Printed in the United States.
Cover design: Scott Idleman
Cover photograph: Queerstock
Text design: Frank Wiedemann
Cleis logo art: Juana Alicia
First Edition.
10 9 8 7 6 5 4 3 2 1

ISBN 13: 978-1-57344-377-7

For Asa,
Bowen Island
cabin boy

Contents

| INTRODUCTION

My first (and among the best) romance: A boy named Jack. Truly, a boy. He was sixteen. His hair was red, his frame was lanky, his nose was prominent. (His nose? Curious, the body parts that attract.) Even now, decades later, tall, wiry redheads with Roman noses—a limited gene pool, to be sure—excite me.

I was a year younger. We lived on a small military base in northern Quebec, fewer than eight hundred people. Schooling ended at grade nine. That's when military fathers and dependent mothers and their children were transferred to another posting.

My life ended the summer Jack left.

Not really. I'm still here, obviously. Hyperbole. But, in memory, it *was* the end of my world. The night before Jack moved away forever, he came to my home for dinner. After, we walked to the woods behind the block of enlisted men's housing where I lived. We held hands. We kissed. We wrestled. We unzipped. We came. We talked about separation and sadness. We cried. We laughed, too—add his swooping laughter to the sweet, sure memory of his red hair and his strong body and his suck-worthy nose. Then I walked him home, to the more upscale, up-the-hill officer's section of the base—individual houses, not row housing. I said hello to his mother and father, whose daily newspaper I had delivered for two years (they tipped generously), and his mother served us leftover crumb cake and chilled lemonade from a kitchen stacked with packed boxes, and we walked up the grassy ski slope behind his house, and we were alone again.

A couple of hours later, he walked me home. Then I walked him home. Then he walked me home. By now the night was deeply dark, our path illuminated by scattered streetlights, a crescent moon, and a blazing canopy of northern-latitude stars. Over the hours we encountered friends, some sneaking smokes on the baseball field, some bicycling, some roller-skating in an era before skateboards. Hanging out. Being teenagers. They slapped Jack on the back, punched his shoulder, the girls hugged him. Good-byes. It was the military. We were used to good-byes.

My parents were asleep when we arrived, again, at my house, but they trusted me, and the military base was a safe village, so our past-dusk strolls caused no concern, and school was out for summer, so bedtime was late. We sat on my back porch, overlooking the forest, and whispered our good-byes. And cried. Then I walked him home, for the last time.

One night, one week, one summer, can be as romantic as a life together.

We corresponded, as promised, but he was the athlete with scant facility for words, and I was the scholar already immersed in words, so his letters soon stopped. He called me once, but he was tongue-tied. In the way of the military, my family was transferred the next year, and we lost touch, my last letter to him returned. Not many years ago, I Googled Jack, but his is a common name.

For all I know, he married, once his acne cleared—perhaps we were just a phase. I was the gay boy, he was sure of me, of us, but he wasn't, back then, in the midsixties, sure of himself. Or maybe he died young, of the disease....

I prefer to think that he found romance, as I have, after that first time with him, with many men, and now with one.

Richard Labonté
Bowen Island, British Columbia

PAWS DE DEUX

Jamie Freeman

Entree (Bishop)

B rooks and I danced a furtive dance for years. We shared a couple of glances, an occasional drink at the bar, even a drunken New Year's kiss, but for some reason we never quite hooked up. We circled, took notice of each other, waited, circled again.

From the beginning, my friend Robbie and I called him "Brooks" in honor of the tailored, buttoned-down Brooks Brothers look he cultivated so assiduously. Over six feet of muscled, hairy perfection squeezed into sleek businessman's drag, gliding past me at a distance.

The night Brooks and I finally hooked up, Robbie and I were standing near the impromptu dance floor in Roger Baldry's living room watching a dozen bears in cowboy hats two-step through a country line dance on the hardwood floor.

"I wish I could dance like that," Brooks said, his lips so close his breath tickled my ear. I laughed nervously.

"I can't remember your name." He handed me his giant paw to shake. "I'm Rick, but I hear you boys call me Brooks."

Robbie pushed me aside, hand held out, palm down like a princess of the realm. "I'm Robbie," he said.

Brooks winked at me. Dark eyes dancing, he bent over to kiss Robbie's hand, his own gestures stiff in mock sincerity. "And your name?" he asked me.

"Bishop," I replied.

I shook Brooks's enormous hand. His brown eyes locked on mine and held me for a long moment. His handshake was firm, his palms broad, his fingers long and thick, engulfing me. His arms were solid muscle beneath the cool cotton of his dress shirt. As he reached toward me, his shirt stretched taut against a heavily muscled chest, nipples poking the white fabric. A tangle of dark hair flashed enticingly where the top buttons of his dress shirt had come unfastened. My pulse raced and my cock leapt. A blush crept up my neck as I realized I had held his hand too long. I took my hand back, but my gaze couldn't leave the tuft of hair, the pulsing vein on the side of his muscular neck, his razor jawline.

"So is Bishop your first or last name?" he asked, baritone voice grumbling, playful.

"It's my first name," I said. "My mother wanted me to go into the priesthood."

He laughed. "Really?"

"Yeah," Robbie interrupted, "but all she did was doom him to a life on his knees." He laughed at his own joke, sucking an olive from a plastic pick and looking slyly into his martini.

"There are certainly worse fates," Brooks said, eyes twinkling.

Later that night, Brooks found me out by the pool. I was sitting barefoot on the flagstones, pants rolled up to my knees, feet dangling in the glowing blue water. Robbie had DUI'd home about an hour before, and I was smoking a joint and letting the dappled water lull me into peace. The music had mellowed with the lateness of the hour; an old Sinatra tune accompanied my quiet mood. "Someone to Watch Over Me."

"Smoke?" I asked, offering him the joint.

He took a long drag and handed it back, kneeling and slipping out of his right loafer. I watched his perfectly manicured hands slide across the smooth leather of his shoe, then peel away the dark cotton sock to reveal molded feet, pale in the glow of the pool lights. The tops were lightly furred, toes perfectly formed, high arches in exact proportion to the rest of his foot. He eased his other shoe off, quietly aware of my attention, smiling and watching my face as he slid the sock over his wiggling toes.

I glanced at him and he raised his eyebrows. *You like?* he seemed to say.

I nodded, took another drag.

He rolled his cuffs up over tight muscular calves, heavily furred and solid as granite, and sat next to me, dangling his feet in the water.

He reached over for the joint again, thick, stony forearm also dusted with dark tracings of hair. My cock stirred.

We smoked in silence. I enjoyed his nearness, the smell of his cologne riding a faint odor of sweat, comforted by his warm breathing presence.

The song changed and Brooks jumped up suddenly, wet feet slapping on the flagstones, water splashing around me. I laughed as he hauled me to my feet and pulled me into his chest.

"Dance with me, Bishop," he rumbled as Sinatra sang the first few lines of "I Won't Dance." We danced slowly in a graceless circle, each clumsily trying to lead, stepping on each other's feet and laughing.

When he leaned over to kiss me, I was so surprised I nearly pulled us both into the pool. His great forearms grabbed me and eased me back from the edge, and his tongue slipped roughly between my lips for the first time.

Adagio (Brooks)

Bishop always tells people we fell in love next to the pool at Roger Baldry's birthday party, and maybe that's true for him, but for me it was a more gradual process. I mean, I know that sounds crass, but I'm not as open to love as he is, I guess. Once burned, twice shy, my best friend Kim always says. But the night by the pool was the beginning of the affair. If melodrama requires us to pinpoint the moment at which the flame was ignited, it was certainly then. I had wandered out to make a phone call (booty call, truth to tell), but when I saw him sitting on the edge of the pool, runner's calves dangling in the blue water, the barest mound of his belly hanging over the waist of his jeans, silvering hair shimmering in the moonlight, I remembering thinking to myself, *Fuck, I gotta get me some of that.* (Bishop is reading over my shoulder now and he just slapped me in the back of the head for that comment, but that's what I thought at that moment.) He was beautiful: broad chest, muscular arms and legs, all packed onto a relatively small frame. A muscle-cub type—thick, hairy, solid, fuckin' hot as hell. So I went over, took a hit of his joint and made a little show of taking off my shoes and socks, rolling up my pants to show off my own muscular legs, and I reeled him right in.

Then the music changed and I jumped up like a fucking idiot Fred Astaire wannabe and we're dancing by the pool, a couple of Russian Circus Bears, circling clumsily and stubbing toes. But we were laughing. Then, when I leaned over to kiss him, I thought for one horrible moment that he was gonna pull me into the pool. I reached reflexively and grabbed him, my fingers wrapping around his rock-hard biceps, and I kissed him, hard and long, like in any old Cary Grant movie, and when we came up for air, I said, "Come home with me."

We got as far as the sofa before I was ripping his clothes off and fuckin' devouring him. The sex that night was incredible, electric. When I slid inside him for the first time, a shock ran through my nerve endings, from the tip of my cock to the crown of my skull; red bloomed behind my eyes, the heat building up under my skin in a rush as potent as a brand-new bottle of poppers. The heat of his asshole sucked me in so far I remember thinking I would tumble inside. My head was swimming, but I recall the two of us bucking back and forth on the sofa, our bodies slamming against each other, sweat pouring down my face, soaking my hair. And when we came, we came within a few seconds of each other, with fierce, throaty growls that made the dogs bark madly, their hackles up with furry outrage. I remember the strain of my ejaculation drained me so much that my arms gave out and I dropped onto Bishop's sweat-slicked back. That's what I remember about the night—heat and sweat and fireworks of light behind my eyes, then the shaky aftermath.

After that night, we saw each other on and off. I think Bishop was working on a gallery show in New York, so he was gone a lot, and I was working on a couple of big government grant proposals, but by Christmas he was back and we were practically living together. And the sex was really good, inventive and kinda frantic in those early years, like we could never get enough of each other. But the moment that really clinched the deal for me was the first time we went up to my cabin in the mountains.

I had inherited a three-bedroom log cabin in the mountains of north Georgia from my father, but I'd only made time to go there a couple of times. Bishop's speculative talk of nights by the fire, hikes in the woods, and sex under the open sky piqued my interest. So we loaded the dogs (his boxer, my dachshund and black Labrador) into the Range Rover (yeah, I know, it's so picturesque) and drove north.

In the afternoons we would hike into the wilderness, exploring nearby mountain trails. One afternoon we were tramping up an overgrown logging road when we came over a peak near the top of a ridge and found ourselves at a breathtaking overlook. I've seen it a hundred times since, in Bishop's paintings, but the artwork hasn't dimmed that one moment, burned forever like a brand in my memory. The ridge dropped off in front of us, a short descent followed by a gentle sloping field of wild-flowers dancing in the breeze. Purple and white flowers flowed a hundred yards across the clearing and splashed against a pine forest that towered in the near distance. Beyond the pines, green mountain ridges ranged across the horizon in every direction. The sky above us was a brilliant blue dotted with white cumulous clouds.

"*Eccolo*," he whispered. Behold.

This man, I thought to myself. *This man, I could stay with forever.*

Bishop jumped three feet down into the field of flowers. I jumped down beside him, turned to him and began to unbutton my shirt.

First Variation (Bishop)

Brooks landed beside me, his face serene, his eyes glistening and affectionate. He unbuttoned his shirt, fingers grappling with flannel and buttonholes. I pulled off my windbreaker and threw it on the ground at my feet. His shirt and undershirt landed on top, followed by my own shirt. He pushed his shorts and boxers down to his ankles, stepping out of them and standing in front of me, a wall of naked muscle and hair with a throbbing hard-on, white socks, and hiking boots. I slid my own shorts off and he pulled me toward him. I kicked my shorts aside, bracing myself against him as we fell onto the pile of clothes and the tumbling ocean of wildflowers.

I landed on his hard chest, forcing the air out of him in a laughing grunt. He grabbed my arms and pulled me hard against him until we were face-to-face, his hot breath grazing my chin, my cheeks.

"I'm gonna fuck you inside out," he whispered.

"If you can hold on to me," I laughed, pulling back in a fluid motion that surprised him. I rolled to the side, feet digging into the dirt, trying to stand. I managed to pull my right hand loose, but he still had a firm grasp on my left wrist. I twisted to the side, trying to break his grip.

He pulled me back on top of him. I rolled again, tried flipping around, twisting his wrist and squirming down his torso. He anticipated my move, and his thick, hairy legs scissored around my waist, long planes of muscle squeezing me tightly, his cock hard against my spine. I ran my hands along his flanks, enjoying hard muscle under hot skin and soft fur. I squirmed, pushing against him. He fought me at first, but when he realized where the alignment of our bodies would place his cock, he let me move unimpeded.

I wriggled until his stiffness slid inside my crack. I swiveled my hips, our body sweat and his ample precum combining in a natural lubricant. A course of shivers rippled through him, his breathing faster and more ragged. His hands were in constant motion, one caressing my belly and chest, the other jacking my cock, slowly at first, then with greater urgency, as his thick cockhead penetrated the pucker of my asshole. With a thrust, he was inside.

"How's that, cub?" he whispered in my ear.

I impaled myself on him, my ass pushing against his muscled abdomen, and then he seized me in a bear hug and flipped me onto my knees, his cock still firmly planted inside me, and rose to his knees behind me. His body flexed and he took control, his hands positioning me, grabbing my arms, my legs, then finally my hips, pulling me into him, setting me up for his pleasure, taking over the rhythm I had set until that point.

His giant hands pulled me close, pushed me away, pulled me back, ever faster, my ass slamming harder and harder against his hips, his cock spreading me open. His right hand was jacking me in time to his thrusts, squeezing me hard, then sliding up the full length of me, his fingers hot from the friction.

Our breathing was ragged. Heat radiated off him like a furnace; sweat coursed down my face, soaking the thicket of fur across his chest. He grunted as if the energy needed to breathe was taxing him, every superfluous movement taking something away from his ferocious pounding. He pumped and jacked. I was close.

"I'm gonna come," he said, before I could make a sound.

His fist tightened around my cock and slammed a few more strokes home before he exploded inside of me, his cum flooding into me. He let loose a deep rumbling roar that seemed to originate between his legs and gain echoing momentum as it burst up through his powerful chest, his throat, and finally into the mountain air. His voice washed me over the edge and I spurted out a steady white stream of cum, finishing the last few strokes myself as he became lost in his orgasm.

We collapsed on the pile of clothes and trampled wildflowers. He stayed inside me, his cock withdrawing of its own slow accord as our breathing slowed and sleepiness overtook us.

Second Variation (Brooks)

Bishop and I napped in the field for a long time, hearts beating a common rhythm, curled together for warmth, until the breeze turned cooler and we dressed to keep the chill at bay. We hiked back to the cabin, hauled some wood inside, and built a fire in the old stone fireplace.

Once the fire was roaring away, we stripped and showered to wash off sweat, dirt and sex. We soaped each other down with an expensive bath gel someone had left behind and stepped out into a cloud of sandalwood-scented steam.

I made dinner while Bishop sat by the fire reading an old paperback mystery. Later, when we were done eating and had settled on the sofa with a couple of Wild Turkeys, Bishop lay back on the pillows and I rubbed his feet. I concentrated on his delicate arch and his slightly rounded toes, rubbing the muscles as his groans welcomed more. I slid my hands up his hairy legs and soon we were naked again, on the hearth rug, kissing each other, the pine-scented candles mixing with peppermint foot cream and the aroma of sex under an early Christmas tree.

Coda (Bishop)

Brooks is on his way back from town. He went to forage for a couple of pints of Chubby Hubby ice cream. We're at the cabin for two weeks to celebrate the tenth anniversary of that party at Roger's house, where we danced to Sinatra by the glowing swimming pool. There's a fire in the fireplace and the mountains outside are covered in a light dusting of early snow.

Anniversaries make me maudlin, so I've been thinking about *us*, about two guys who stumbled into something lasting. We have a marriage of sorts, though neither of us would ever call it that. No rings, no flowers, no ceremony, no vows. We'll never be two tuxedoed grooms sharing a spotlight dance at our reception, or feeding each other pearly white wedding cake. But neither will we be the couple that brings home a third to spice things up, or argues over a houseboy, or hammers out complex ground rules for sexual polygamy (touch this, but not that; do this, but not that, and only if I'm there too). And yet, despite the fact that we don't fit either tradition, we've choreographed moves that work for us—a couple of sweaty, basketball-playing, rock-climbing, football-watching, foul-mouthed, cigar-smoking, whiskey-drinking men, who happen to be unaccountably, unabashedly in love with each other.

When I think about what we have, I recall my grandparents, who forever laughed with each other like newlyweds, drank bottles of red wine with dinner, sang old Gershwin songs to each other on special occasions, and always waltzed together at family reunions.

I don't remember my grandfather very well, but my grandmother outlived the love of her life by about twenty years. She spent a couple of those years living with my mother and me, usually absorbed in one of her two remaining passions: old paperback mysteries or black-and-white movie musicals.

One night when I'd just turned sixteen, the two of us were sitting at the old Formica table in my mom's kitchen. It was late, one or two in the morning. My grandmother was chain-smoking and drinking coffee from a mug shaped like an owl. There was an *Ellery Queen* on the table, spine bent to mark her place, and Fred and Ginger were twirling around on the television, the music soft beneath the sounds of the ceiling fans and my grandmother's smoky breath. She leaned forward and said, "Bishop, your grandfather used to say marriage is like a mystery. You keep looking for clues and hoping for the best."

She took a drag from her cigarette, eyes drawn away from me to the TV. "But he always had a flair for dramatic pronouncements, even if he knew they were wrong. There's nothing mysterious about marriage. Marriage is a dance. You choose your partner and sometimes you stumble or you can't find your rhythm, but sometimes," she pointed her nicotine-stained fingers across the room, "sometimes it's just like that."

We watched Fred and Ginger twirl around the room, he in a tuxedo, she in a stunning low-cut black dress, hands and feet and bodies perfectly aligned, a perfection so simple, but so stunningly beautiful. My eyes teared up.

"'Smoke Gets In Your Eyes,'" she said.

"I guess so," I mumbled, wiping my tears.

She looked at me for a long moment, taking another drag on her cigarette. "Huh," she said when she finally exhaled, then got up to refill her coffee mug. "Some things last, Bishop. Not every lovely flame dies," she said, reaching for the powdered creamer.

I look now at the fire blazing in the fireplace and hear the truck tires bouncing along the gravel driveway outside. I walk over to my iPod dock and scroll through the list. Sinatra. "I Won't Dance."

I meet Brooks at the door and peel his jacket off muscular shoulders. I reach for the buttons on his flannel shirt, working my way from throat to waist.

"You're gonna make me drop the ice cream," he laughs, kissing me on the neck.

"Dance with me, Brooks" I say.

He smiles broadly, pupils wide in the half-light, and steps into the music.

WORLD'S GREATEST DADS

David Puterbaugh

The overstuffed armchair in the corner of the store was the color of honey butter, the same color as Winnie the Pooh. The couple stood over the chair and stared at it, arms folded across their chests.

Mark, the taller of the two by half an inch, took a step forward and grasped the arms of the chair. He pushed it slightly to the right, toward a sleigh-shaped crib, and then stepped back and refolded his arms. Scott stood beside Mark and nodded his head, on top of which sat a faded blue *New York Mets* cap speckled with dried dots of paint, the same almond-color paint that covered the four walls of their new nursery. Mark turned and reached for an embroidered *Noah's Ark* pillow that rested on the seat of a nearby rocking chair. He placed the pillow in the center of the armchair, fluffed it, and rejoined his partner. The two men studied this new combination, but Scott shook his head, and a moment later, after Mark agreed, Noah was returned to the rocker.

"What about Noah?" Scott said.

Mark's attention was elsewhere. "Huh?"

"I said, what about Noah," Scott repeated. "Do you like that name?"

"Look at my face," Mark said, his eyes still on the chair. "Does it look like I like that name?"

Scott studied him. "No, you look like a homeless guy just sat down next to you on the subway. And farted." Mark tried not to laugh but a small grin escaped.

"What about a celebrity baby name?" Scott asked.

"You mean, like *Apple*?"

"Of course not. Apple is a girl's name."

"Apple is not a girl's name or a boy's name," Mark said. "It's fruit."

"So Kiwi is off the table, is that what you're saying?"

It was a Saturday morning, and the store they were shopping in had been open for less than two hours. Store employees wearing cooks' aprons with their employer's name embroidered across their chests moved about the floor busily—fluffing and folding, sweeping and stocking—before the rush of the afternoon crowds.

Mark swatted the brim of Scott's cap. "C'mon, what do you really think?"

"Of Kiwi? I was only kidding."

"Not that, what do you think of the chair?"

Scott shrugged. "It's okay, I guess. Kind of expensive for a nursery though, don't you think?"

"It's no more expensive than any of the other furniture we've looked at."

"Still, you do realize with all the money we're spending on just one room we could have bought the kid his own place, right?"

The sun streaming through the twelve-foot-high windows lit up the furniture in the store like sets on a stage. Soft jazz played over the sound system at an unobtrusive volume, unlike the grating music now coming from a pair of nursery mobiles— which Scott was mischievously winding up—subjecting them, as they waited for the salesclerk who was helping them to return from the stockroom, to the dueling melodies of "Hush Little Baby" and "Twinkle, Twinkle Little Star."

"I think it would look great by the window," Mark said, lowering himself gently onto the chair. "I can see us taking turns sitting in it, giving the baby his bottle, watching the sun come up."

"I can see us cleaning baby puke off of it," Scott said, bending down to examine the price tag. "Do you think they'll tell us how to do that?"

"Our baby is not going to puke," Mark said. "Our child is going to be perfect. What about Dakota?"

"Now I'm going to puke."

"Be serious."

"I am serious, Dakota is awful. What about Edward?"

Mark shook his head. "Too old."

"What do you mean 'too old'? I thought Edward was your grandfather's name?"

"Exactly. Are we having a baby or a senior citizen?"

Scott moved around the sleigh-shaped crib to a bookshelf, where a dozen or so overpriced children's books were neatly stacked. He pulled out one with the ironic title, *My Very Own Name*. "What about Christian? I've always liked that name."

Mark shook his head again. "Too red state."

"Jesus," Scott said, flopping down on the arm of the chair.

"That's definitely too red state," Mark said, pushing him off. "What about Toby?"

Scott turned and looked down at the man he had spent the last five years of his life with, the man he had shared his deepest desires and dreams with, the man he called his partner, his lover, his best friend. "Are you insane? Because you'd have to be to stick a kid with two gay fathers with a faggy name like that." Mark began to argue but was interrupted.

"I! Want! To! Ride! It! *Now*!" A child of about four raced down the aisle in front of them, expertly dodging oncoming stock clerks and a rather large chaise lounge, which two store employees were preparing to move from a display on a furniture dolly. The same could not be said for the child's mother, who wore high heels that were clearly not made for running. She was unfairly weighed down by two armloads of shopping bags.

"Isaac! The escalator is not a toy! You have to hold Mommy's hand!"

The boy's mother slowed herself further when she decided to climb over the chaise lounge rather than go around it, losing a shoe and half the contents of one of the bags in the process. "Isaac! Do you hear me, young man?! *Hold Mommy's hand!*"

Scott couldn't help laughing. "What about Isaac?"

Mark smiled. "Too Jewish."

"Too Jewish? *You're Jewish!*"

"That's my point. Do you really want to be in a store someday yelling 'Stop right there, Isaac Cohen!' People will think we're chasing after a rabbi."

"Isaac Hanson Cohen," Scott corrected him. Mark made another face. "Uh-oh," Scott said. "Now you look like the homeless guy kicked off his shoes."

"This shouldn't be so difficult," Mark said. "We had no problem choosing a girl's name."

"Nope, no problem at all," Scott said. "Not until we found out our little Julia was going to be born with a penis."

"You know what the real problem is, don't you?"

"What's that?"

"We've slept with too many guys."

"What? We have not."

"Yes we have," Mark said. "We both slept around way too much when we were younger—" Scott rolled his eyes.

"Don't shake your head," Mark said. "Are you forgetting how we met?"

"People hook up online all the time," Scott said. "That doesn't make us sluts."

"But it does make us promiscuous, and now our child will pay the price for our promiscuity."

"Are you kidding me? Can't you hear how ridiculous that sounds?"

"Be honest," Mark said. "How many boys' names have you said no to because you dated a guy with the same name?"

Scott paused a moment. "Define 'dated.'"

Mark narrowed his eyes. "More than a hookup."

"Oh, you mean a whole weekend."

Mark got up from the chair. "If you're not going to take this seriously—"

"Okay, okay. A couple, I guess."

"A couple." Mark held up his left hand and began counting off. "Alex, Brian, Christopher, Daniel, *Ernesto*."

"What a minute. Did you make a list? *And memorize it?*"

"That's just the beginning of the alphabet," Mark said. "Add to that all the guys I've been with and you know what we're left with?"

"The letter *Z?*"

Mark looked defeated. "Make jokes, that's what you're good at. I can hear the neighbors now. 'Oh, look! Here come those two man whores and little baby no name!'"

Scott sighed loudly. "Why do you always have to be such a drama queen?"

"Why can't you ever take anything seriously?"

"Babe, I am being serious."

Mark nodded his head and turned away.

The entire second floor of the store where Mark and Scott were shopping was dedicated solely to furniture, but the first floor—home to the gift registry department, where Mark and Scott had registered for a catalog's worth of gifts prior to their wedding two years earlier—was a wonderland of houseware accessories. Here amongst the colorful assortment of coffeemakers and stand mixers, table lamps and flower vases, shower curtains and bath towels, the couple had selected the stovetop griddle that Scott now used every Sunday morning to make his world-famous pancakes, the enamel-coated stockpot for Mark's chili—Scott's favorite meal—the four hundred thread-count cotton percale sheets that Scott kicked off their bed every night (where Mark awoke most mornings to find his partner lying beside him, face-down and shirtless, like a wrestler down for the count), and the digital photo frame that displayed their favorite pictures in high-def succession—shots of their families, their vacations, their dog—a continuous slide-show of their life together.

The second floor housed the furniture, which was sectioned off into dozens of professionally designed "rooms," each separated from the other by imaginary walls that customers could pass through freely, each room more enchanting than the last. There was a sitting room that appeared tailor-made for a seaside cottage, dressed in a casual white linen sofa, sky blue throw pillows, a colorful wall print of a solitary beach, all accented with the obligatory ship-in-a-bottle on its mango wood coffee table. Beyond this was a bedroom that made its section of the store feel like a forties-era Hollywood soundstage with sleek, stained veneer Deco nightstands and an oval dressing room–style mirror mounted on the wall. At its center was a marquee-worthy, button-tufted headboard, covered in a smoky gunmetal fabric.

Scott wandered across the aisle into a "living room," a space that was designed to resemble a Manhattan loft. There was an L-shaped, mahogany leather sectional sofa, and in front of it an enormous, round coffee table, which appeared to have grown up out of the green wool rug it rested on like the stump of a once mighty tree. Across from the table was a sleek television console, and on top of it a faux flat-screen TV. Scott slumped down onto the sofa and resisted the urge to put his feet up on the table.

Mark had wandered off as well, to a bedding display at the center of the floor. The blanket that caught his eye was a chenille throw in a masculine shade of green. It was soft to the touch as he ran his hand across it, like a child's stuffed animal. Mark pulled the blanket from its shelf and unfolded it, and then carried it back to the corner of the store where the nursery furniture was displayed.

Scott watched Mark fold the blanket lengthwise and drape it across the back of the armchair. Despite their words he had the same feeling now that he'd had this morning, when he found Mark on a stepladder in the nursery, and watched him from the doorway as he stenciled the alphabet along the top border of the walls. It was a feeling that dampened his eyes, a feeling that made him want to get as deeply inside of Mark as humanly possible. It was a feeling best described in one word. *Home.*

Mark considered the price of the blanket before glancing in Scott's direction. Scott had put his head back on the sofa and pulled his cap down over his eyes. The way he looked now reminded Mark of the past Thanksgiving at his sister's house, when Mark's four-year-old nephew had begged Uncle Scott to watch *How the Grinch Stole Christmas* with him after dinner. Mark had taken a picture of the two of them later that evening as they sat together on the couch in the family room, Scott with his hat pulled down over his eyes as it was now, his nephew asleep with his head resting on Scott's lap. If they were at home Mark would have taken the blanket and covered him with it.

As Mark gathered up the blanket to return it, a man in his thirties came down the aisle toward them, accompanied by two small boys. The man was wearing an untucked oxford shirt rolled up at the sleeves, and he was pushing a double stroller. He was listening to the older of the two boys, who appeared to be about three years old, as the child walked beside him, talking animatedly while hanging on to the side of the stroller. Seated in the stroller, next to a woman's purse and a very large diaper bag, was the second boy, who was no more than a year old. The man had thick dark hair that he wore short, and a fair complexion. Except for his glasses the two boys were the spitting image of him.

"Daddy, shoe untied!"

The man looked over the stroller at the older boy's shoe. "Again? We've got to practice some more, pal. Don't you want to learn how to tie your own shoes like a big boy?"

"No!" The boy raced to a nearby sofa and climbed up on it.

Seeing this, the boy in the stroller began to wail. The man sighed as he turned to his younger son with his older son's shoe in his hand. "You want to get out? You're just going to fall down again."

But the little boy persisted, and held his arms up over his head. The man pushed the stroller up onto a rug beside the sofa and lifted the little boy out. "Don't say I didn't warn you. Hold on to the stroller, buddy."

Mark stopped to watch the scene play out. Scott was listening too and had one eye open under his cap. The man got down on his knees in front of his older son and had a hand on the back of the little boy, until he realized he would need it to get the shoe back on the older boy's foot. He checked his younger son, then took his hand away and quickly began tying the shoe. As he did this the older boy leaned forward suddenly and looked over his father's shoulder.

"Daddy! Liam's walking!"

"What?" The man whipped his head around. Scott pushed his hat up and sat up straight.

Mark held the now perfectly refolded blanket to his chest. The little boy had let go of the stroller, and they all watched as he took two steps toward his father on tippy toes with a big smile on his face.

"Go, Liam!" the man said. He caught the boy just as he was about to topple over.

The man stood up with his son in his arms and smiled at Scott and Mark. "Did you guys see that? My kid walked!" His smile then quickly faded into a look of sheer panic. "My wife's going to kill me." At this the older boy collapsed back onto the sofa in a fit of laughter. "Funny daddy!" he said.

"You look good there." Mark stood in the aisle across from Scott after returning the blanket.

"It's comfortable," Scott said. He patted the seat beside him.

Mark walked around the enormous coffee table and sat down close to Scott, their sides touching. "In all seriousness," Scott began. He reached down and took Mark's hand. "Do you know what I see when I look at you now? Broadway quality costumes for the school play, brown bag lunches that will have all the other kids begging to trade, birthday parties so elaborate

Martha Stewart will want to throw in the towel. Our kid may not have a name, but he's never going to forget yours. *Dad*."

Scott brought Mark's hand up to his lips and kissed it. "You're going to be a great one."

Mark squeezed Scott's hand back. "So are you, funny Daddy."

"Don't worry, we'll come up with something," Scott said.

"I guess there's always the Bible," Mark said. "There's bound to be dozens of names in there we haven't considered."

Scott straightened up. "I'm sorry, did you say *the Bible*?"

Mark's head hit the sofa cushion. "Why?" he asked wearily. "Are you going to tell me now that you've fucked a guy named Ezekiel?"

The salesclerk who had been helping them earlier reappeared amongst the nursery furniture. He craned his neck as he looked about the store, searching for his customers.

"Over here," Scott said, waving his hand above his head. He and Mark stood up as the clerk hurried over to meet them. "Sorry that took so long," he said. "I thought you were still over there."

"We've been on the move," Scott said.

The salesman laughed politely. He was young, in his early twenties, and shorter than Scott and Mark. There was a slight twang to his voice that suggested he was not a native of the Northeast. And his smile was not something he had acquired that morning at a team meeting before the store opened to customers, but genuine. The salesclerk handed Mark a fabric swatch.

"I'm happy to report we have the Addison chair in stock. If you gentlemen are interested in purchasing the chair today I can have it shipped to you by the end of next week."

Mark rubbed the fabric between his thumb and forefinger and looked at Scott.

"It's up to you," Scott said.

Mark turned to the salesclerk. "We'll take it."

"Wonderful!" the clerk said. "If you'll just follow me over to the counter I'll be happy to fill out the paperwork for you."

Scott began following the clerk but stopped when he realized Mark wasn't with them. He turned around. "What's the matter?"

Mark stood frozen in place, the expression on his face one of sheer amazement, like that of a child who has just seen the Magic Kingdom for the first time. "His name tag," Mark said. "Did you see it? I can't believe I didn't notice it before."

"No, I didn't see it," Scott said. "What's his name?"

Mark rushed to Scott's side and spun him around. They were both now facing the counter. With a huge grin on his face Mark put his arm around Scott's shoulder, as Scott read the sales clerk's name tag. And smiled.

Nicholas.

TEMPLETON'S IN LOVE

Jerry L. Wheeler

The line curled around the block like a pubic hair, I typed in my head.

Maybe not the most effective simile, but writing porn for a living leads you to make some weird comparisons. And the line *did* stretch all the way from the new faux red brick front of Carmine's Supper Club and Ristorante down to their landmark sign a block and a half away. But even landmarks change. The flowing script of the old *Carmine's* logo had been replaced with a blocky Bodoni whose straight, modern design was almost as offensive as the pretentious RISTORANTE squeezed in at the bottom.

This part of Colfax had always been the hip, trendy district, but the patchouli-fragrant head shops and musty used bookstores had been replaced by gourmet ice-cream stands and chain coffee shops with parking spots for strollers and dogs allowed on the patios. The only survivors were Sailor Jack's Tattoos—now known as BodyArt—and Carmine's.

I stepped out of line long enough to gauge the distance to the front door: about fifty or sixty people away. I hoped they wouldn't sell out. Templeton hadn't played in ten years—I *had* to be there. Seeing him without Stan would be strange, but Stan and I hadn't seen each other for ten years either. I was wondering if I should get two tickets, and who I could ask to go with me, when a familiar face emerged from the front door and began walking the line, stopping occasionally to talk to someone.

It was Carmine Jr., looking a little older than when I'd last seen him. His face brightened with recognition when he approached. "Tom!" he said, grabbing me in a bear hug. "How *are* you, buddy? How come we never see you down here anymore?"

"I'm good," I said as we separated and looked at each other. He'd filled out nicely, acquiring the stocky barrel chest Carmine Sr. had, tufts of hair sticking out of the collar of his white shirt. "I moved out to the burbs—don't get to the old neighborhood much. If I hadn't gotten your flyer, I wouldn't have known about this."

"Flyer? Wow, I didn't think the homeless guys I hired got out that far."

"Your folks still around, or are you running the place now?"

He chuckled. "They say it's mine but Mama comes down to the kitchen every day to tell me what's wrong with my red sauce, and Pop's usually behind the bar buying drinks for his buddies—you know how it is." He handed me a piece of paper. "Here's a discount voucher. It'll save you some cash when you get up to the window. I want to make sure the old crowd gets in to see Templeton."

I shook my head. "I can't believe he's playing after what—ten years? He's got to be in love again. Did you talk to him?"

"Pop did. All I know is that I had to get the piano out of

storage and have it tuned. He's gonna be here for one show, tomorrow night—Hey, are you still with Stan?"

I knew he'd ask. "No, not since Templeton stopped playing."

"Sorry to hear that. You guys were a good couple." He looked down the line. "I gotta finish handing these out," he said. "Look, when you get here tomorrow, hunt me down. I won't have a lot of time to talk, but I'll make sure you get a good table. If it wasn't for the old crowd coming to see Templeton, we never would have made it through some pretty lean years. We want to treat you guys right. See ya, buddy." He clapped me on the shoulder and continued his trek down the line.

The old crowd, I thought. Our crowd. Stan and I had seen a lot of the same faces every Saturday night—mostly other gay men, dykes, and goth kids with bohemian aspirations, but once word spread, young straight couples started driving in from the suburbs looking for emotional diversions they couldn't find at the multiplex. Carmine always found tables for us, though—tables for dreaming of the someone Templeton sang about, tables for falling in love and tables for breaking up.

And, always, in front of the stage, sat his partner, Taylor, his bulky frame as out of place at their small table as a stuffed bear at a dollhouse tea party. He was as big and tall as Templeton was short and skinny—opposites who attracted attention. They lived in the neighborhood and Templeton was an accountant. That's all anyone really knew about them. No one knew how they met or when their birthdays were or even how Templeton had started playing at Carmine's. We didn't even know his first name.

You could spend dinner talking to them, as Stan and I had on a few occasions, and be as clueless by dessert as you were when the salads came. Taylor parried direct questions effortlessly as Templeton smiled, his skinny face full of piano-key teeth, and told another isolated anecdote unrelated to the subject at hand.

They were a world unto themselves, and they never handed anyone a map.

But Gershwin was in their world—Gershwin, Cole Porter, Rodgers and Hart, Dorothy Fields, and Jule Styne. "Nothing past nineteen-sixty," Templeton used to say, "when music became vulgar." And he sang those witty, urbane songs of love and loss directly to the man at the front table, who looked up at the stage with admiration. He played them all for Taylor. Everyone else just happened to be in the room.

Then Stan and I started falling apart. Arguments and tantrums and nights of silent disgust for each other kept us away from Carmine's for a couple of months. When we went back for an attempted reconciliation dinner, Taylor had lost a shocking amount of weight. AIDS, cancer—who knows what he had? The rumors ran rampant. Templeton still sang to him but a shrill desperation crept into his voice, as if the melody could keep Taylor alive. And we resumed our regular Saturday night attendance, as if it could restore us as well.

But in the end, it didn't work for anybody. Taylor died, Stan and I broke up, and Templeton stopped singing. Carmine tried out a few other acts, but it wasn't the same. And then the small stage was gone, replaced by a few more tables and a coffee station in the back of the room. I moved to the suburbs to hide and write.

Now, Templeton was playing. He *must* be in love again.

The box office was getting closer—only a few more people now. I stepped around the legs of a homeless guy sleeping against the wall. His head was tilted to the right, slumped on his shoulder as he snored out a foul stink of unbrushed teeth and stale wine.

Homeless man sex, I thought. *That'd be great for the collection of fetish stories I have in the works.*

It didn't do anything for me personally, but someone would be bound to get off on it. I noted his craggy, unshaven gray jowls and the stains on the thighs of his tan work pants, forcing myself to look higher at the slight bulge of his crotch and trying to imagine his unwashed cock smell. I stepped closer, hoping no one would notice me trying to sniff a homeless guy.

"Tommy? Is that you?"

Even if I hadn't recognized Stan's voice or the way he called me Tommy, I would have known by his presence. I'd been feeling it since I stepped in line. I figured he was around somewhere—he *had* to be. I hadn't let myself look for him because I dreaded seeing him as much as I longed to. If we were supposed to see each other again, he'd have to find me. It was his responsibility. After all, he was the one who left.

"If you have to ask, I must be." I couldn't help but smile when I looked at him. He always made me smile. What would we do now? An awkward hug that reminded us of what we used to mean to each other—or even worse, a tepid handshake? What do you say to someone whose last words were "Fuck you"?

Stan solved the problem by stepping in with a combination hug and clap on the back, heavy on the reassuring clap part. I mirrored his actions, trying to ignore his scent, which I loved—a combination of aftershave and pheromones that always drove me to sniff his pillow long after he'd left our bed. He broke away first, holding me at arm's length by the shoulders.

"You look great," he said with a broad smile.

"So do you." It wasn't a lie, at least on my part. Stan used to be geek-chic, tall and skinny with a nose the size of Idaho and deep-set blue eyes. But somewhere between "Fuck you" and "Tommy, is that you?" he'd grown into his nose and put on a few pounds. None of it looked like fat, either. He'd had his teeth fixed and was wearing an Armani sports jacket over a gleaming white shirt, expensive-looking jeans and loafers that looked too buttery soft to be domestic. Corporate law must have been good to him. And Connie.

"Thanks, buddy." The "buddy" sounded too foreign, too straight to be coming out of his mouth. "I can't believe Templeton's playing again after all this time. He must be in love again."

"I was thinking the same thing."

"How many, please?" The girl's face was irritated and expectant. She held a wad of tickets and a finger poised for counting. How long had I been standing in front of the window?

"Are you going?" I asked Stan. It was a reflex action.

"I wanted to, but it looks like the line's pretty long. I just got here."

I turned back to the window and reached for my wallet. "Two, please," I said, handing over the discount voucher Carmine had given me.

She snapped the tickets off a roll and took my money. "*Next.*"

"Does this mean you're taking me?" he asked as we stepped away from the window. I handed him his ticket

"I just gave you a ticket, didn't I?"

"Maybe you'd rather take your boyfriend or partner or whatever."

"Nope." I tried not to say it like I hadn't been on a date in five years.

"Great," he said. "I'm looking forward to it. Hey, how about you come over and see my place, Tommy? It'll shock the hell out of you when you see where I'm living. Or do you have to get back home to the boyfriend?"

Two "boyfriends" in two minutes, I thought. This from a guy

who couldn't even *say* the word ten years ago. "Sure," I replied. "Let's go."

He took the lead as we crossed the street against the light, a weird air of expectant hesitation between us. We both wanted to talk, but how to start? True to form, I let him begin, content to admire the gray in his hair and the lines on his face. They made him look even more handsome than ever. I had always imagined they would.

"So, how have you been?" he finally asked.

"Good—and you?"

"Can't complain."

"How's Connie?"

"Don't know. Haven't talked to her in a long time."

"What happened?"

A half smile crept across his face. "What you said would happen. How did you know?"

"I didn't. I mean, I thought…okay, it's what I *wanted* to happen. But at least she had the baby. You got some of what you wanted."

"Nope. She lost it, and the doctor wasn't optimistic about trying again." He fell silent for a few seconds, staring away as if another life of his was off in the distance. "We thought about adopting," he said, looking at me again, "but our lives seemed too tentative after that. After a couple of years, we got tired of making each other miserable and packed it in. She lives somewhere in Portland now."

"I'm sorry to hear that."

"Why? Portland's nice," he said with a grin.

"No, no—I'm sorry to hear you split up."

We paused at a curb, letting traffic go by as he squinted into the sun. "Why should you be sorry?" he asked. "I walked out on you—on *us*. You should be raging, but you're sorry instead."

The cars cleared and we crossed Colfax. Just like Stan to tell me how I should be reacting. "I don't do rage very well," I said, shrugging. "Anyway, that was a long time ago."

"You're too nice, Tommy. You always have been. You know, I was the luckiest man alive, but I fucked up. I walked out on the only person who ever really loved me."

"Connie loved you."

"Not like you did. And you know what? I've never loved anyone like I did you. I can't believe I was stupid enough to throw it away. We could have had a beautiful life together, but you're probably settled down with some nice guy in the suburbs. Dogs and a mortgage and everything."

Who the hell was I walking with? Stan the Contrite? Stan the Apologetic? I wished I could think fast enough to invent a fantasy husband, but he always knew when I was lying. "I do live out in the burbs, but I'm single. I haven't been on a date in, like, five years. Sad, huh?"

"Sad? I think it's a damn shame. You don't know how many times I picked up the phone to call you, Tommy."

"Why didn't you?"

"I wasn't sure if you'd hang up or not. You know I'm not good with rejection."

"Who is?" I replied before thinking.

He was silent for a few moments. "I guess I deserved that."

I hadn't meant it like that, but nothing I could have said would have convinced him otherwise. Letting him think whatever he needed to, I walked alongside him. The route was disquietingly familiar—two blocks south of Colfax and east one block on 13th to Sherman. When we turned south again, it hit me.

"You rented our old apartment," I said.

"No," he said quickly. "I rented the one across the hall. When Connie and I got divorced, I needed a place to stay, and I've always liked this neighborhood. When I was down here looking, I ran into Madeline. She told me there was a vacancy, so I took it. That's all."

Too many coincidences and too much denial, I thought. I didn't know what was going on, but it was cute rather than menacing, so I decided to let things play out—and despite the weird vibe, I was enjoying being with Stan after all this time. There was a reason I'd never fallen for anyone else.

We walked down Sherman toward Poet's Row, a series of apartment buildings named after famous poets, and stopped in front of the Robert Frost. The entry door had been refinished and some of the brickwork redone, but it was as charming as I remembered. Virginia creeper laced the eaves and framed the second and third floor windows, shadowed by huge elms that were just starting to drop leaves.

When we stepped into the entry hall, the sight of the mailboxes and the scent of mildewed carpet and wood oil took me back twenty years. We were young and in love and just coming home from a walk around Capitol Hill, fresh and energized by talking and walking. And horny. God, we were so horny then.

I had to touch him. The feeling was so instinctive and automatic that my reaction surprised even me. As he dug in his pocket for his front door key, I reached up and began massaging his shoulders. He stopped, straightened up and leaned back into me, the pressure of his body making me want to press myself into him even more. But I couldn't. I had already gone way farther than I intended.

I tried distracting myself with the distance between us those last weeks, remembering his "Fuck you, Tommy" and how I crammed our pictures into a cardboard box without even taking them out of the frames, sobbing as they crashed to the bottom of the Dumpster in the alley. And how I slammed the lid down on the whole broken mess, swearing I'd never let anyone do that to me again.

"Mmm, that feels nice," he said. And the past all disappeared into his breath and his smell and his voice and his flesh giving way beneath the flex of my fingers. He turned his head toward mine, his eyes closed and his lips parted. They looked soft and warm, exhaling a ragged passion as familiar to me as my own. All I had to do was lean forward a few inches and throw myself off the cliff again.

That's why I let go. His eyes popped open when we broke contact, and he sighed. I may have too. I can't remember. All I remember is instant regret. "I can't," I think I said.

He nodded, his lips closing around a rueful smirk. "I know. I'm sorry."

But I knew he wasn't.

"You still want to come in for a few minutes?" he asked.

"Sure," I said, not sure at all.

I followed him down the hall, going farther back in time with each step until I got to the door of our old apartment. I felt the heft of the suitcase I left with and I swore if I'd looked at my palm, the imprint would have been there like a stigmata. Stan must have noticed me staring at the door.

"It was pretty weird for a while," he said. "Now, I don't even notice it. C'mon in." The floor plan was just like our old place except turned around—same arched doorways, same radiator, same vaulted ceilings with the same ceiling fan. "Want something to drink?"

"Water would be great, thanks." Glancing around the room, I noticed a general shabbiness. The carpets were worn, the sofa fabric shiny and frayed in spots, unrefurbished second-hand furniture. Not the surroundings for a successful corporate lawyer. "So, how far is this from your office?" I asked, sitting on the sofa.

He came back from the kitchen with two bottles of water. "I don't have an office," he said as he handed me one and sat down beside me. "I'm not doing corporate law anymore."

"Did you retire or what?"

"Eh—bought some properties, sold 'em, made some money. Don't do much of anything anymore. I'm trying to live simply. Do you remember the day I left?"

"Parts of it."

"I'm sure you remember the 'fuck you' part—you don't know how sorry I am about that. But do you remember what you said right before that?"

"No." It wasn't a routine denial, either. I really didn't.

"You said I'd never be happy until I learned to live in my own skin, and you were right. Well, that's what I've spent the last five years doing—learning to live in my own skin. I'm in therapy, I came out to my sister and my folks and, believe it or not, I'm happy for the first time in my life."

"No more hiding, huh? Feels great, doesn't it?"

"It *does*," he said, "but I only have one problem."

"What's that?"

"I miss what we had." He moved so close our knees touched. I was up against the arm of the sofa and had nowhere else to go.

"You'll find it with someone else," I replied, holding my bottle of water as if that would ward him off.

He moved in even closer. "I don't want someone else," he said. "I want you."

Stan took my head in both of his hands and guided it to his lips, but I already knew the way. His smell and the touch of his fingers on my cheeks rendered me helpless. Our lips met in a soft, speculative kiss that soon became eager and definite. I

put my arms around him and he let go of me. I was in his grip
anyway.

Dizzied by the frantic dance of our tongues, each kiss-muffled
sigh cast me farther and farther back, into a warm, safe place
I knew well but never hoped to see again—and it was just as
beautiful and narcotic as I remembered it. We waltzed danger-
ously close to the edge of a precipice without a rope to pull us
back to reality. I had to stop the music in my head, no matter
how much I liked the tune. "I can't do this," I said, pushing
away from him and getting up from the sofa. My lips already
felt cold and deserted. "I can't go back."

"It's not going *back*, Tommy," he said, a pleading I'd never
heard before in his voice, "it's going *on*. Right from where we
left off."

I didn't want to argue the point. I couldn't. "I have to get out
of here," I said, heading for the door.

"Wait, Tommy—don't…"

But it was too late. I was already out in the hall. I felt something running over my hand and realized I was squeezing the
water out of the bottle I'd been holding. I wiped my fingers off
on my pants and dropped the bottle on Robert Frost's carpet,
fighting my way to the front door through a flood of memories.

I must have taken that ticket out of my pocket a thousand times
trying to decide whether or not to go. By the next afternoon, it
was smudged and torn a quarter of the way through due to a
hasty decision after a few vodka and tonics that were supposed
to put me to sleep but didn't.

Staying home with yet another drink would have been the
easiest thing to do—let it all pass me by and forget the whole
damn thing. But I couldn't. If I could have forgotten it, I wouldn't
have gone down there to pick up the ticket in the first place.

It wasn't Templeton, it was Stan. It wasn't over between us—maybe not in the way *he* thought, but I had things to say and he needed to hear them. Or at least I needed to say them. I wasn't about to get back together with him, that was for sure. He might be in therapy, he might be sorry, he might even love me, but I'd moved on. Too bad he hadn't.

That was in my stronger moments. Other times I wondered just what I'd moved on to—an empty house? Meals alone by the television like my widowed dad? Not going to the symphony because I hated going places by myself? I needed to make more friends, but I didn't socialize well. I'd never acquired that skill.

I don't know if it was curiosity, fate or the unfinished business with Stan, but Saturday night found me standing outside Carmine's with my smudged, half-torn ticket in my hand watching a lot of people file in but none coming out. Hoping Carmine Jr. would make good on his promise to find me a table, I straightened my tie, brushed lint off my jacket and went inside.

The main dining room was packed, and so were the two new overflow rooms off to either side. They had the same burgundy carpet, dark wood paneling, maps of Italy and framed pictures of Frank Sinatra on the wall. *There must be an Italian Restaurant Warehouse that every Carmine's, Angelo's and Dino's in the country buys this stuff from*, I thought. But the new rooms also had video screens and speakers.

"Hi, Tom," Carmine Jr. said, coming around from the reservations desk. "Glad to see you. We weren't sure if you were gonna make it."

"We?"

"Follow me—your table's this way." He zipped into the main dining room, quickly weaving his way down front between tables, waiters and customers. I almost lost him in a near collision with a family-style platter of pasta primavera, but I was able to catch up with him when he stopped for a crossing dessert cart. He motioned me closer to the stage and pointed to a small table with a huge bouquet of flowers. Stan occupied the other chair.

"Don't ask if I have another table," Carmine Jr. said. "It's here or the alley. You boys talk. I'll have Stephanie take your cocktail order. It's on me, so drink up—I'll be overcharging you for dinner." He smiled. "Enjoy."

"I'm glad you showed up," Stan said. "I would have looked pretty stupid sitting here with these flowers and no date— wait, maybe I shouldn't have called it a date." His grin was as disarming as ever, bringing to mind some of the crazy stuff I used to do to see that grin.

I had to smile. "I think this qualifies. Thanks. They're beautiful."

"And," he said, moving them between us and the rest of the room, "I got them big enough to hide everyone else, so it just seems like it's us and the stage. I hope the waitress knows we're back here."

I couldn't banter without speaking my piece first. "Look, I'm sorry about running out on you yesterday."

"I'm sorry about springing it on you like that. I should have warmed up to it first, but you know me—I'm pretty direct."

"Yeah," I said. "I remember. That's why I'm going to try to be the same. I know how you feel, believe me. And if this had come right after we broke up, there would be no question about giving it another shot. But it's just too long, Stan. Too long. And I'm not sure it's what you really want."

"What do you think I want?"

"I think you want to take back ten years, Stan. You can't do that. I mean, look what you're calling me. No one ever calls me Tommy anymore."

I thought I saw a tear in his eye but it could have been a trick of the light. "But that's how I remember you."

"See? That's the problem. I'm not that guy anymore."

"I don't believe that," he said. "Do you mean to tell me the man who enjoyed romance more than anything else in the whole world is gone? What happened to him?"

"He starved to death," I replied. "We can be friends, Stan. I'd really like that. I enjoyed spending time with you yesterday. Let's just be friends, okay?"

"I'm not sure I can do that," he said as the waitress appeared over the flowers.

"What can I get you gentlemen to drink?"

As we gave her our drink orders and requested two house specials for dinner, the dining room lights flickered on and off, finally settling on dim as the crowd began to buzz.

A familiar figure walked briskly from the bar and took the stage. Templeton hadn't changed much. Always small and thin, he'd gotten even thinner. His brown eyes looked hard and flinty. His moustache was still black, but his dark hair was flecked with gray and wrinkles grooved the corners of his mouth.

He closed his eyes and breathed deeply for a moment, then brought his hands to the keyboard and began to play "Come Rain or Come Shine" softly. He hummed in a barely audible voice until he'd played the verse through, then he sang out. His voice was lower, more hoarse than I remembered it, but it had a gravity that wasn't there before. Finishing the opening number, he ignored the enthusiastic applause and swung into "Misty" without a break.

His voice was getting stronger, swooping and swirling sassy through "Ain't Misbehavin' " then vamping on the melody to segue into a soft, seductive version of "Mean to Me." He was in great form, as if he hadn't been away from Carmine's for ten years. I always loved his piano skills because I seemed to hear more notes than he looked like he was playing. But as terrific as his performance was, it was different—lonelier. It needed joy.

The audience lapped it up like heavy cream. The warmth they exuded in return filled the room, but Templeton remained unaffected by it. He neither acknowledged nor discouraged the attention. He let it wash over him—a wave of devotion that crashed against the stage and pooled uselessly beneath the pedals of the piano.

He continued playing for an hour, moving from song to song without a break for even a sip of the Calistoga water sweating atop the piano. Stan and I were mesmerized. Neither one of us said anything during that hour, despite the arrival of our dinners. We ate, but I don't remember a thing about the food.

The only pause in the set was before the last number. He took his fingers off the keyboard and nearly drained the Calistoga dry in a couple of swigs before leaning into the mic. "This is something I wrote many years ago," he said, "for someone who never got a chance to hear it."

He began a soft, sad intro of minor keys bespeaking major heartbreak. There were no lyrics, only a slow, desolate melody that rendered words insufficient. The middle was stronger, more hopeful, but it was only a thirty-two bar oasis that lingered long enough for relief before the chord progression turned somber and elegiac once again. I realized then that Templeton was *not* in love. It would have been impossible to invest that tune with that much pain, that much sorrow, if he had been in love. Why was he performing again, then? Was it a tribute to Taylor? Some sort of closure?

Toward the end, the melody simply drifted off. Templeton played it softer and softer until it disappeared like bitter smoke over the crowd. In the silence that followed, I heard sniffling and saw many people daubing their eyes, including Stan. Without waiting for applause, Templeton left the stage and walked quickly to the bar area, disappearing behind a door in the back. He must have heard the crowd's deafening appreciation. I clapped so hard my hands hurt.

"He's not in love," Stan said as we sat back down. "There's no way. I mean, he was great, but there was no joy."

We still thought alike. "I was thinking the same thing. You remember he used to say he couldn't perform without it. That's why he quit when Taylor got sick. So, why is he up there?"

"Mr. Tom?" said a creaking, accented voice. It was Carmine's mother, Rosa, standing inside the tubular aluminum cage of her walker. She had to be in her eighties. She was wrinkled and stooped, her black and red dotted dress draped in folds over her tiny frame. Her pulse beat through the paper-thin skin of her wrist as she held out her hand. I stood up and clasped it.

"Rosa," I said, "how are you? You look terrific."

"I look old," she cackled, "but it's okay. At least I don't look dead." She glanced down at our empty plates. "*Mange bella*— the special, it was good?"

"It was great."

"Grandmama Cochelli's red sauce, it don't miss. Carmine learns pretty good, but I make tonight. Good to see Mr. Templeton back, eh?"

"It certainly is—he sounded great."

She broke out in a white, dentured grin. "Beautiful," she said. "He got to have a little bit *Italiano* in him, eh? Ah, is just too sad what happened."

"I know. I still think about Taylor to this day. He was a wonderful guy."

She knitted her gray eyebrows with confusion. "Mr. Taylor, yes. He always make me laugh—but Mr. Templeton..."

"Templeton?"

"He has the cancer too."

I felt the blood drain from my face. "Oh, my god," I said, "we had no idea."

"He don't say nothing to nobody, but he hurts. I see sometime when he comes in the morning to practice for tonight. You should stop at St. Catherine's and say a novena for him before you go home. For him not to hurt so much."

I really couldn't speak.

"We will," Stan said for me. "Thanks for telling us."

"You are good people, so you should know. Nice to see you again, Mr. Tom. *Buona notte.*"

"I don't get it," I said. "He's dying, but he's playing again."

"I think you have the order wrong there," Stan replied. "He's playing *because* he's dying. He's anticipating seeing his joy again."

The lights dimmed again and Templeton emerged, taking the stage a little less adroitly than before. Or maybe it was my imagination. He sat down at the bench and began to noodle through "Come Rain or Come Shine" again. The audience fell quiet, but this silence wasn't the expectant one that had preceded his first set. It was the solemn, respectful silence that ensues after an unsettling disclosure.

Either from the wait staff or Carmine Jr., the news of Templeton's illness had spread and he definitely noticed the difference in the crowd. He continued playing with the song, running down the same sixteen bars over and over as he gazed out on the audience with a thoughtful frown.

Suddenly, he seemed to understand. His playing became more purposeful and the frown vanished, replaced by the thinnest of grins as he bent down to the mic. "Oh, I see," he said. "But you shouldn't feel sorry for me. I'm not sorry. It's the second best thing that's ever happened to me." He played harder, staring straight up as he crooned the verse loud and clear.

He could have been looking at the water-stained ceiling or he could have been looking at God, but we knew who he was looking at. My gaze went up there too for a respectful moment, but there was nothing for me in that direction. I looked at Stan, then I took his face in my hands and kissed him as hard as I could, thinking that maybe sometimes you have to go back before you can move on.

CLOSER TO
THE SKY

G. A. Li

It was different here at night, tall grass shifting in the shadows and the river rushing in, black and wild before it picked up the glow of the fire. Weekdays hardly anyone else bothered, and Jake liked to ride out with his paints and his brushes, his easel on his back. He'd set up about half a mile down river, usually, but he liked to come up this way sometimes, too. It felt more like home than his apartment, one room over the hardware store in town, dusty books and old photographs, a kitchenette, notes stuck in random places. Out here there was honeysuckle and clover and flat gray stones in the riverbed, cold beneath his feet. Out here Jake could forget about all the things he couldn't remember.

He hadn't planned on being out here tonight, but someone had pressed a hand-drawn card into his hands at Finn's night before last, and right after that Tommy had followed him through the parking lot, sliding into his truck and jerking him off slow and dirty, murmuring about flyboys and fallen angels and the fiery taste of Mary Lou Miller's pussy, back in the day.

He didn't much care about Mary Lou Miller one way or the other, but he was going to come anyway, Tommy's voice in his ear and Tommy's hand on his cock, his thumb sliding over the slit just right, making his hips buck up hard. He was still trying to catch his breath when Tommy ran his fingers through the spunk on his belly, gathered up as much as he could and used it to jerk himself off, too, his mouth open and his legs spread wide. Moonlight was shining through the windshield, turning Tommy's skin pale blue, and Jake wouldn't have looked away right then for all the memories in the world.

It seemed fitting that Mary Lou Miller was here tonight, too, smiling and laughing, dark curls loose around her face, dancing up against some boy at the edge of the bonfire's glow. Jake didn't recognize him right off, the slope of his bare shoulders and his khakis hanging low, but he sure looked pretty enough from here. Everyone looked pretty from here, Jake thought. It was the firelight, and the smoke shine, too; hazy and sweet, sparks in the air and crushed grass underfoot, Tommy singing softly, strumming his guitar.

Jake made his way toward Tommy roundabout, Sadie Harris's warm hand in his for a while, twirling away and spinning back again, her body soft against his, her earrings sparkling in the night. Jake took a joint from Billy Zee's thick fingers as he passed them by, and Sadie kissed his cheek and danced away, taking Billy with her. Tommy caught his eye and licked his lips, and Jake smiled, looked up at the sky.

Anything was possible on a night like tonight, with the river and the fire, home brew in dark bottles, the stars shining bright. Tommy said, "Sit for a minute," and even now Jake knew how Tommy's minutes turned into hours and he sat anyway, close enough to feel the heat of Tommy's skin, different from the heat of the fire. Tommy's heat was like the air and his voice like the smoke, raspy and sweet, curling into Jake when he breathed.

Tommy leaned close and Jake blinked real slow, smiling as Tommy *tsk, tsked* and lifted Billy Zee's joint from his fingers. Jake had turquoise-blue paint caked into his cuticles, yellow ochre smudged across his wrist. He had scars he couldn't explain yet, smooth skin that tingled and itched across the front of his shoulder, the back of his thigh, his hip. "These are our friends," Jake said and Tommy nodded, picked out a new rhythm on his guitar.

"You remember this one?" Tommy asked, and Jake hummed a little, shook his head. He did and he didn't.

Tommy's eyes were green and gold and he had freckles all over, the same color as his hair; he liked strawberry ice cream, and mayonnaise on his fries, and he could fix anything with a motor, anything at all. An unconquered wolf was tattooed on his bicep, a burst of red, white and blue inside his elbow from when he first joined the Guard, a trail of shamrocks on his side that twisted way down low.

Jake had a trail of shamrocks, too. He didn't remember getting them, but he knew they were there, could imagine him and Tommy driving into the city back before Jake took off for flight school, Tommy's fingers in his hair, his lips kissed dark and swollen, both of them reeking of beer and whiskey and laughing their asses off, toasting the luck of the Irish. Jake imagined that a lot, especially in the shower, his fingers tracing over the shamrocks, thinking about Tommy, the way he'd taste, the way he'd feel, wet and slippery, the way he'd sound with Jake's dick buried deep inside him and his breath caught up in his throat.

Fuck, Jake thought, shifting uncomfortably, his dick hard, trapped between his belly and his briefs. Tommy strummed his guitar and his voice sang out, and Jake tried to think about something else.

"It wasn't like this before," Tommy said softly, setting his guitar aside to run his thumb over Jake's bottom lip and kiss him slow, one hand on the back of Jake's neck holding him close. "With us, I mean. I didn't know if you knew."

Jake closed his eyes, leaned into Tommy's touch. He didn't know what they'd been like before, but from the way his brain filled in the missing pieces he thought he must have wanted Tommy even then, couldn't imagine ever wanting anything else. He remembered Tommy in ways he couldn't explain, details and dreams and fleeting faded images. He felt safer around Tommy than around anyone else, like he was okay again, like Tommy was cool with him even if he wasn't the same guy he'd been before the war. "Does that matter?"

"Not to me," Tommy said, and just then someone threw a log on the fire and the embers popped, sparks flying in the air. One of the girls squealed and out of the corner of his eye Jake could see Billy Zee wrap his big arms around her, could hear her laugh, sweet and high, could hear him laugh, too.

Jake's hands were sweaty, hot on his thighs, and Tommy's eyes were on his, leaning in to kiss him, his fingers spread on Jake's jaw, his throat. Jake's body knew how to do things that Jake didn't remember learning—he could tie a knot in a fishing line without thinking about it, cast out over the water and make the fly dance just so; he could drive his old truck no problem; hell, he could climb into the cockpit of a fighter and fly her just fine, not that anyone would let him. Not anymore.

Tommy bit at Jake's lip, sharp and teasing, soothing the bite with his tongue before licking his way back into the kiss. Jake heard himself moan and it sounded sexy even to his own ears, and he knew his body remembered fucking, remembered it well.

His hips pressed closer, Tommy's mouth on his, his hands, the heat in the air and the river rushing by, the scrape of stubble against his throat.

He pulled away just enough to see Tommy's eyes, his flushed cheeks, and his smile as he picked up his guitar. It was easy, being here like this, and Jake leaned back and closed his eyes, listened to the night close in around them. Sadie Harris sat down beside him for a while, ran her fingers through his hair. She stood up to leave, kissed Tommy's cheek and climbed into Billy Zee's arms, and when Jake looked around again it was just him and Tommy, the fire burning low.

"I want you," Jake said, and it was simple enough, Tommy's smile against his, the way his eyes crinkled up at the corners. He liked to think he'd been smoother before, had known the right thing to say, to do, but Tommy was smooth enough for the both of them, Jake thought, because Tommy's fingers were curled under the hem of Jake's shirt, dragging over his stomach, his ribs, Tommy's mouth following close behind, hot lick of his tongue, scrape of his teeth, and Jake had meant to be self-conscious about this, about his scars, about his body, about the way the dark head of his dick was already poking out of his jeans, but he couldn't be, not now, not with Tommy leaning right up against him, spreading their shirts out on the grass behind them.

Tommy's dick was hard against Jake's hip, soft denim right there, slick skin everywhere else, his voice raspy in Jake's ear, "So fuckin' hot, you have no idea," and with the way he looked, Jake's back on the grass and Tommy above him, the last of the firelight in his eyes, in his hair, Jake thought he might be right.

"Tommy," Jake breathed, and Tommy kissed his way down Jake's body, his palm pressed over Jake's fly, tongue darting out to taste the slick trail of precome on his belly before he wrapped his lips around the head of Jake's dick, hot and wet and Jake couldn't help rocking his hips a little, couldn't help the flex of his fingers on the back of Tommy's neck. "Fuck, Tommy."

"Yeah, later," Tommy said, grinning a wicked grin, popping open the buttons of Jake's jeans and tugging them off his hips, knuckles sliding over the scars on the back of his thigh, making Jake shiver. Tommy kept one of his hands right there, palm open, fingers splayed wide, and Jake tried not to squirm. Tommy shifted lower, rubbed his cheek on Jake's belly, in the crease of his thigh, stubble scraping over the shamrocks, his mouth pressed to the lowest one. "You remember these?"

"Luck of the Irish," Jake whispered, and Tommy bit his lip and swallowed hard.

Jake tensed, wondering, but Tommy just shook his head and laughed real low, his eyes flashing bright as he licked up the length of Jake's dick and sucked it back down. Jake wanted to flip them over, feel the weight of Tommy's cock in his mouth, nudging at the back of his throat, wanted to taste him there, lower, everywhere, and then Tommy's calloused fingers were in his mouth, earthy and smoke-sweet, then gone way too soon, and Jake could hear himself moaning way up high, needy sounds he couldn't stop, Tommy's fingers circling his hole and pressing in, spit-slick and rough, so different from his own.

Jake leaned up on his elbows, scrubbed his hand through Tommy's hair. "Tommy, fuck, c'mon," and Tommy let Jake's dick slip out his mouth and slap wetly against his belly. Jake was breathing hard and Tommy was, too, his skin flushed and his lips swollen, his fingers in Jake's ass twisting slow. "Christ, were you always this much a tease?"

"Yup," Tommy said, grinning. He still had his jeans on, and that was wrong in ways Jake was too dazed to really think about, but Jake could see how hard he was at least, could see where the head of his cock pressed against the faded denim, leaking. "Been teasin' you for years."

"Yeah?" He wasn't sure if that was true or not, but it didn't matter. This was what mattered, what he had now, what he could touch, taste, remember. "Huh."

"Sure took you long enough to notice."

"Hard not to, now," Jake said. He pulled at Tommy's jeans, buttons popping open and Tommy's dick jutting out, shiny at the tip, red-gold curls dark around the base. Tommy shifted to his knees, mumbling "Sorry, sorry," as he wiped his fingers on their shirts, dug a rubber out his pocket and tore the packet open with his teeth.

Jake reached for it, but Tommy shook his head, rolled it on himself. "Too close," he whispered, leaning in to brush a kiss across Jake's lips, his hips pressing Jake's thighs open, his cock sliding in the hot crease of Jake's ass. "Tell me you're ready."

Jake wrapped his hands around his thighs and hitched them higher, the blunt head of Tommy's dick against his hole, rub of Tommy's hand against his skin guiding it in, thick and hot and bigger than his fingers, better, Tommy's mouth on his, sweat dripping from his forehead, pressing in slow, slow, Tommy's hips twisting, both of them moaning low.

Jake swallowed hard, wished he could see Tommy's cock fucking in and out of him, wished he could see his body stretch to take it, and then Tommy shifted, kneeled up and angled Jake's hips high, and fuck, it was so good like this, the slow burn and the impossible heat, his hips rocking up and up, Tommy's hand wrapped around his dick just right. Jake knew he wasn't going to last, was going to come just like this, too soon, his shoulders pressed into the ground and Tommy's cock in his ass, thrusting deep.

He bit down hard on his lip, on his fingers, but he couldn't stop it, hot splash of come on his belly, his chest, Tommy cursing low and breathless, his voice hoarse and his hips losing their rhythm. "Fuck, Jake, fuck." It still felt so goddamn good, so right, fireflies in the tall grass and the stars overhead, slow buzz in his blood and Tommy fucking him hard, leaning over, "Gonna make me come," his mouth pressed against Jake's throat and Jake's fingers twisted in his hair, in the hot well at the base of his spine.

"I missed this, last tour over there," Tommy said later, his dick soft and sticky on Jake's stomach, his knees tucked up against Jake's ribs. Jake nodded, imagined he probably missed this, too. "We learned to fish right here, back when we were kids," he said, smiling, his fingers tracing the scars on Jake's shoulder, certain, like he was playing his guitar. "You remember?"

Jake shook his head, ran his thumb over Tommy's bottom lip, and Tommy laughed, licked at rough edges of Jake's nail, the soft pad of his skin. "I just remember you," Jake said, watching Tommy's eyes light up, listening to the river. It was different here at night, Jake thought, but not so different. It still felt more like home than anywhere else.

THE ABBEY

David May

The speaking in a perpetual hyperbole is comely in nothing but in love.

—Frances Bacon

When one is injured, one withdraws.

There are wounds to lick, memories to purge, and revenge to plan. So it was with Storm, now abandoned by a lover who had promised him Forever—Forever apparently being his private code for Until I Meet Someone New. The worst part of it was that Dale was so ingratiating, full of smiles and promises of future talks and of finally taking a weekend away together. Yet when the door shut, Storm heard that familiar inner voice reminding him that Dale was all charm, adequate sex, and nothing more.

"I just can't live with a poz guy, baby," had been Dale's excuse; but this was an unreliable excuse for a man who refused to be tested and never balked at taking Storm bareback.

Storm was the son of hippies who had embraced his queerness with disturbing enthusiasm; queerness was embraced, but the future (other than the current crop of organically grown herbs) was left to itself to sort; and so, with his limited education, Storm knew he was lucky to be working at Nordstrom's. Alert as well as queer, he had a critical eye when it came to quality, fit and value—but only in regard to men's haberdashery and never in regard to the objects of his affection. When it came to men, he was a romantic, relying on the written word for his reality check. Consequently, he was frequently disappointed. Storm was, if not handsome, almost pretty, with dark hair and eyes, thick lashes, pale skin and full pink lips that ought to have been a girl's. This brush with beauty attracted the men he sought to know, though his judgment regarding them was consistently poor.

Packing up his belongings before moving to his new apartment, he came across the trove of pornography that Dale had denied was his, pornography for which he proclaimed a deep revulsion. Storm looked through the old *Drummer*s and *Honcho*s but felt no such disgust—in fact, his manhood took an instant move north, and soon he was pitching a tent in his worn sweats. Storm lay back on his bed and reached for his erection. Spitting in one hand, he stroked his uncut manhood, sliding the foreskin back and forth over the gland, while turning the pages with the other: images of men in distress, stories of boys tricked into slavery, drawings of godlike men fucking similar, albeit smaller, godlike men. In minutes he splattered cum all over himself and the wall behind him. He let the jizz run down and stain the wall, leaving his mark on what had been Dale's apartment.

A few minutes later, he was out the door. Storm had not paid the rent when it was last due, knowing that the only reputation this nonaction would sully would be Dale's, since the lease had been in his name. On Dale alone would hang the stigma of an abandoned apartment with rent in arrears. Shutting, but not locking, the door behind him, Storm felt his revenge had been exacted, even if its repercussions would be unfelt for some time. The stack of offending periodicals he took with him.

Storm read his trove of leather porn and wondered where he might get more. Going online, he discovered that people collected it, and through those collectors he met men who could answer his questions:

Q: *How much of this is real, how much fantasy?*

A: *All of it is fantasy, some of it made real by mutual consent.*

Q: *Do I need to do all?*

A: *No one does everything. Don't believe the hype.*

Q: *What if I change my mind midstream?*

A: *If you're not absolutely sure, don't start.*

Q: *How do I meet guys who will want to do what I want to do?*

A: *I notice you live in Seattle. Want to meet?*

A stone dropped in Storm's stomach. At the same moment his balls pulled up and his manhood hardened. Alone and naked at his computer, he spat on his turgid prick and stroked it, being careful not to let it splatter on the keyboard.

Storm arrived on time, straight from work.

He'd passed by the street-level condo the night before while on his usual Saturday night sojourn with his friends, passed by and lingered at the door and wondered what lurked within the well-lit home; two cats sat in the front window and looked at him with frank curiosity. Then he noticed the name of the condo development: the Abbey, an odd name for a new building in a town where the fashion ran toward names like Brix, Vertigo, Zen, and Press.

He was still in his suit. He wondered if that would bode poorly for him, if he oughtn't to be in torn jeans and boots. Would this mean the end of any chance to be initiated into what, he was sure from his reading, was a secret society with secret hand-shakes and obscure hankie codes? He scratched the stubble on his face: at least he was scruffy, as was the fashion and so accept-able within the hallowed confines of Nordstrom's. He knocked at the door; the stone returned to the pit of his stomach even as his phallus oozed excitement. *What would happen to him now,* he wondered. *Would he pulled in by his hair and thrown to the ground? Forced to his knees to lick the man's boots and suck his mammoth* (for Storm assumed it must be mammoth) *man root, choking on it with tears running down his face?* Fear filled his eyes while his balls pulled up close in their excitement. Would he be raped and beaten, or…?

One could always hope.

The door opened.

The man was neatly bearded with a gentle face and kind brown eyes; he was of medium build and dressed in jeans and faded red pocket T. His feet were bare. He smiled when he saw Storm, offered his hand.

"You must be Storm. I'm Brad. Please come in."

Storm took the offered hand, admiring the salt-and-pepper beard, the warm smile and the kind brown eyes.

"Yes. Thank you."

Brad motioned to the adjoining room.

"Have a seat. Wine?"

"Yes, please."

Storm remembered the arcane and complex etiquette from the stories he'd read in the old copies of *Drummer*, the many

transgressions made by the unwary—and worthy of punishment. Should he really sit down? He had been told to, but just
to be safe, Storm waited for his host. He looked around the
room: about what one would expect this side of Capitol Hill,
cozy but not too small, with an open plan, high ceilings and
double-glazed windows. The furniture was new and modern,
suiting the space. Art was sparingly displayed where it could
best be appreciated. A single bookcase overflowed with books,
some jammed in; Storm looked at the titles, hoping for clues of
what was to come.

Storm almost jumped when a cat rubbed against his leg.

"Don't mind Moose. He just wants to introduce himself. His
brother is around somewhere, too. Please, sit."

"Thank you."

Storm took the offered wine and obeyed. *Should I have said,
"Sir"?* he wondered.

"So, you came straight from work?"

"Yes. I hope that's okay. I didn't want to be late and I didn't
have time to change, so I…"

"Where do you work?"

"Nordstrom's."

"I thought you looked familiar. The picture on Facebook
doesn't do you justice."

Storm blushed.

"Storm is an unusual name," Brad said, stroking a second cat
that now sat next to him.

"My parents were hippies," Storm said by way of an apology,
making room for Moose on his lap. "We lived on Vashon
Island."

"You can push Moose away if you want. You'll get his hair
all over your suit."

"It's okay. We had a house full of animals on Vashon."

Brad laughed. "Of course!"

There was a pause in the conversation, one fraught with meaning, the moment he'd dreaded and feared, the moment when—

"So, you're curious about it all."

"Yes. Sir. Yes, Sir."

Brad smiled.

"Not yet, baby. This is just an interview. Calm down."

"Oh, okay, to see if I want to do—with you?"

"Maybe. But it's really more about whether I want you or not."

"Oh."

Storm blushed, the stone dropped in his stomach anew, and his hard thickened manhood leaked salty honey. Was this the transgression? Was this moment when—?

"It's okay, baby. Nothing's cuter than a nervous boy afraid he'll say the wrong thing."

Storm's trousers were suddenly too tight.

No plans were made when they parted. Brad shook his hand again and said they'd be in touch. Only his lingering hand in the small of Storm's back, when he opened the door, hinted that there might be more.

Storm would have to wait, but he wondered for how long. The stories he'd read gave him no clue. It might be hours or days or weeks or months, all spent in turgid anticipation, days spent in longing, nights spent listening for the steps of booted feet coming from the shadows, a rustle in the bushes, masked figures coming at him from behind in an alley when...

He heard from Brad less than a week later, finding a message on his voice mail suggesting dinner. Storm called back and suggested eight o'clock somewhere cheap. Brad agreed with a gentle chuckle that matched Storm's memory of Brad's kindly brown eyes.

Storm arrived late, this time in jeans, apologizing for his tardiness. Brad stood and shook his hand.

"No need to apologize, baby. Dad will remember it later."

Storm flushed, his blood draining to his tumescence.

"Yes, Sir," Storm managed to say, looking up at Brad's smiling face, at the friendly eyes with a mischievous glint. Brad reached across the table and stroked Storm's face, caressing the stubble. "By the way, I have a special thing for scruffy boys, especially when it suits them."

Storm smiled.

"Thank you. Sir."

Brad offered to pay for the pub dinner but Storm insisted on going dutch, though he wondered if that broke some cardinal rule he'd not read about in *Drummer*.

"Then you have to let me buy you a drink."

He put his arm around Storm and led him up Pike Street to the Eagle, the bar where Storm had never dared tread for fear he might be assaulted, raped, forced to his knees and made to suck manhood after manhood, forced to swallow all their seed until...

Brad opened the door, paid their cover, and ordered their drinks. The doorman greeted him, as did the bartender. Storm looked around, slightly disappointed that the Eagle was more a neighborhood bar than anything else. There was some leather, yes, and some middle-class men dressed in Carhartts and Doc Martins attempting to affect a working-class demeanor. Brad disturbed Storm's reverie with the drink. They leaned against the bar, clicked glasses, and bent their heads together so that they might hear each other over the din of the music. Brad kept his arm around Storm as they talked of nothing, caressing Storm's shoulder with a firm hand, a hand that moved its way up to

Storm's neck and pulled him into a kiss.

Storm almost dropped his drink; he felt his knees buckle, felt the need to drop at Brad's feet and lick his boots (only he was wearing canvas walking shoes) and offer himself to his new Master.... Instead, he lost himself in the kiss that went on for minutes but felt like hours. He clung to Brad's frame for support, sought more from the kiss than he had imagined possible, receiving it in kind, giving as much as he took and offering more. Brad broke the kiss, pulling Storm away by his hair, pushing him to his knees. There was a smattering of applause that Storm hardly heard as he knelt on the floor, looking up into Brad's warm eyes. Brad smiled, spat in Storm's face and handed him his drink.

"That'll do, pig."

When they got back to the Abbey condo, Storm was neither raped nor tortured, much to his initial disappointment. Rather he was made love to while bound, his hands shackled to the headboard. Blindfolded, Storm gave in to the ravishment, the sensation of being played with by one who sought to know his body. There were kisses, licks and bites, slaps and caresses. His response to each was noted for future reference. Storm made noise, groaned and cried out, let the gods know where he was, lost in the darkness of this new and exquisite agony. Dale had always told him to be quiet during sex; Brad encouraged Storm's cries of joy, of delicious abandonment. Only when he felt his legs being lifted onto Brad's shoulders did he pause to say:

"I'm poz, Sir."

"I know."

Brad entered him in one smooth motion, one steady thrust. Storm threw his head back, yelped like a dog that had been startled awake.

"Oh, Sir, oh, Sir, oh, Sir…"

Storm rolled his head back and forth, unable to contain himself. Having never known abandon before, he succumbed to the sudden assault, the gloved hands that smacked his ass, chest and belly, that smacked him hard across the face as Brad's breath got shorter and faster.

Suddenly Storm felt Brad's face next to his.

"I'll only ask you once, hole," came Brad's urgent voice. "You want it?"

"Yes, Sir! Make me your bitch, Sir. Please, Sir, please, Sir, please!"

Brad howled and pulsed inside Storm, filling him with holy semen, with the communal fluid of men. Storm sighed in relief: now he belonged to Brad.

The next morning over coffee, Brad looked at Storm with a critical eye, as if assessing Storm's worth, or perhaps his own expectations of what might come. His gaze made Storm nervous.

"Sir? Did I do something wrong, Sir?"

"Not at all, my boy. You did everything right. Which is what bothers me. If we go on, I'll have to decide whether or not to collar you, but I won't collar you unless… That scares me, boy. I was only planning on showing you the ropes and sending you out on your own."

"I don't know what to say, Sir. Should I go?"

"After you tell me about last night."

"It was not what I expected, but more than anything I hoped for. Please tell me that this is just the first step, Sir."

He slipped off his chair and knelt at Brad's feet.

"Please tell me I can continue, Sir. Please train me and make me yours, Sir." Storm's eyes filled with tears.

In response, Brad leaned down and kissed his eyes, tasted the tears that clung to his thick lashes.

"Okay, Sir. I need to go home and get ready for work, Sir. May I be excused, Sir?"

"Go on, boy. I'll pick you up when you get off."

"Thank you, Sir."

Storm kissed Brad's hands, got up and left. Brad watched him walk away and whispered: "Damn you for being so damn perfect."

Just before Storm finished his shift, Brad walked into the store, his eyes lighting up when he saw Storm. Storm smiled back, relieved, having spent the whole day distracted, wondering what he might have said but didn't, what he shouldn't have said but did, going over each moment of that morning trawling for clues.

"Boy."

"Sir."

"Ready to go?"

"Yes, Sir. I'll be right with you, Sir."

A few minutes later they were walking up Pike Street, holding hands.

"What's next, Sir?"

"We date, boy. We date, and I teach you how to make me proud."

"Yes, Sir. Thank you, Sir. May I tell you what I hope, Sir?"

"Of course, boy."

"I never believed that this could happen to me, but now it seems in reach, Sir."

"What's that, boy?"

"To be owned, Sir, to wear a man's collar."

"We'll work on it, boy. Let's not move too fast."

Still, as they held hands heading into the Eagle, they knew where they were heading, or at least where they wanted to go.

* * *

Storm was held through the night, his hands bound in front of him. He fell asleep with an erection he'd been forbidden to touch, and woke at least once during the night being penetrated by Brad. In the morning his hands were freed and he was allowed to cum while Brad entered him yet again. Brad, for his part, was unable to leave enough seed in Storm to satisfy himself. Each coupling marked Storm as Brad's own; and Storm knew this, knew that he was becoming what he wanted to be under Brad's hand, knew that he wanted to belong to the man piercing his soul as well as his body.

Done with their lovemaking, they showered together—watched with fascination, if not acute concern, by Moose and his brother. Brad fed the cats and the men went to breakfast on Broadway, holding hands the whole while, Storm only addressing Brad as "Sir," Brad calling Storm "boy," though Storm was only ten years his junior. But when Storm had to leave Brad for work, retail knowing no weekend, the parting kisses were close to tearful, leaving Storm with a sense of a yawning emptiness deep in his gut where Brad's semen had been so liberally spilled.

How long to wait? he wondered. Dare he call, send a note or an email? He scoured his ancient copies of *Drummer* for clues. The etiquette described was complex, and often contradictory. As best as he could figure out, he should wait expectantly for Brad's call (whether literally or figuratively) but was in fact under no obligation to any obeisance since Brad had not locked a collar around his neck. Similarly, he might, on seeing Brad at the Eagle or the Cuff, kneel in front of him in the hope of being acknowledged, but must not expect more than a nod on the street. Storm gritted his teeth with frustration.

As often happens in these instances, it was only when he had finally calmed down a few days later and was, while hopeful, no

longer anxious, that he left Nordstrom's after an evening shift
to find Brad waiting for him, flowers in hand. Storm blushed;
no one had ever brought him flowers, and he accepted them
demurely. They were hardly out of the store, it seemed, before
Brad pushed Storm against the wall and held him in a lip-lock
for several minutes, Brad's tongue reclaiming Storm as his vessel,
crushing the flowers between them. Storm wanted to swoon,
and he was not sure from his reading that it wasn't appropriate
at times, though this hardly seemed like the time or place.

Suddenly tearing his mouth from Storm's, Brad grabbed his
hand and said, "Come on, baby. Daddy's taking you to dinner."
Storm followed him, crushed flowers in tow, to Pine Street where
Brad hailed a cab.

That night Storm was taken into a large, mostly empty, walk-
in closet where a bolt had been secured to the ceiling. Stripped
naked, Storm's arms were secured to the bolt and a belt was
taken to him. Storm's body twisted and turned in anticipation
of each stroke, his back arching as his head rolled back and
forth. Between strokes there were caresses, kisses, whispered
encouragements. Storm lost himself behind the blindfold, ached
desperately for each touch, whether the belt or the hand, that
might guide him back to Sir and the safety he offered. Hardly
any sound escaped his lips, and it was not until Storm's beatific
expression turned suddenly dour that Brad knew Storm had
passed the precipice.

He held Storm close, kissed him and caressed him, before
releasing him. Storm collapsed into Brad's arms. This, Storm
thought, was when it might be all right to swoon.

A few weeks later, Storm awoke bound, Brad's arms around
him, with the quiet certainty that he was in love—albeit not

desperately as he'd hoped he might be, ravished again and again in a dark dungeon where no one would ever find him or hear his cries. Rather, he was quietly and calmly in love. He had no need to declare it, only to enjoy it. *Life is sweet*, he thought, even as he was flung onto his stomach and taken without ceremony. Through it all he smiled, almost humming a tune when Brad pushed his spent manhood in Storm's mouth so that he might suck the final drops of seed from it. He said nothing, made no declaration to Brad or the world, or even to Brad's cats.

"I think," said Brad, untying Storm's hands, "that you're ready to show off at a dungeon party. I'll be able to really whale on you, so you'll have to promise to make me proud."

"Yes, Sir. I promise. If I can, Sir."

Brad looked at him critically.

"I appreciate your honesty, boy, but a simple 'Yes, Sir' will do. You have to trust Dad, because you, baby boy, can go much farther than you've gone so far."

Brad kissed him, held him close.

"Yes, Sir."

"When was the last time I let you cum, boy?"

"Last Sunday, Sir."

"That long? Balls must be getting blue."

"Yes, Sir."

Brad stroked Storm's erection, gently slapped Storm's balls.

"Good."

"Yes, Sir."

Storm wanted to ask for permission to cum, but decided it was better not to broach the subject lest he be punished with a lashing, or, worse, tossed onto the street naked, his clothes flung behind him. That Storm had never been punished in his life, beyond the occasional time-out or deprivation of television privileges by his parents, left him with a simultaneous sense of awe and trepidation at the possibility of punishment. He did not know how punishment would differ from the flogging he'd received the night before, but he knew it would be different and, accordingly, unpleasant. He did not want to think about it.

Wearing only a too-tight pair of leather shorts that Brad had procured for him, he went to the kitchen to make coffee. He prepared Sir's cup, a dollop of milk and no sugar, and brought it to him, kneeling at Sir's feet as Brad stroked his hair and face.

"Pretty boy."

Storm cast his eyes downward and blushed.

"Thank you, Sir."

"That'll do, pig."

"Sir?"

"Go get yourself a cup of coffee and relax, boy."

"Yes, Sir."

Storm rushed to obey, but sat back on the floor next to Brad's chair when he returned. Whether or not he had permission to sit on the furniture, he preferred the floor next to Sir. Brad stroked his face and hair again, as if verifying for himself that Storm was both real and worthy of his affection.

Brad sighed and Storm's attention refocused on Sir; he held his breath in anticipation of what Sir might say next; but Brad said nothing, only smiled and opened his newspaper.

The next Saturday night Sir called a cab to take them to the other side of town, to the much-anticipated party. They arrived at an unremarkable house, one that was neither pristine nor shabby, and entered without knocking. Men in leather lay about the living room while hopeful, uncollared boys sat on the floor vying for their attention. Only the collared boys, fewer in number, had the satisfied smiles of the well beaten, secure of their place.

Storm stripped off his sweats as ordered and stood naked

except for his leather shorts. Wordlessly, Brad secured a leather collar around Storm's neck. Ignoring Storm's excited sharp intake of breath, he attached a leash to the collar and, greeting those he knew, led the way to the basement playroom. Keeping his hands behind his back as if they were bound, as he knew they soon would be, Storm glanced discreetly about him, looking for clues about what was to come, listening for the cries of the damned as they were tortured deep within the subterranean depths, screams of agony, of euphoric abandon...

The playroom was pristine if small. Those not playing milled quietly about in the adjoining room, respectful of the intimate transactions taking place nearby. They waited for a space to become available, for an elaborate bondage scene to disentangle itself. Brad sat back on a couch, talking to friends as Storm knelt, hands behind his back, eyes to the floor—as he had read boys in his position were supposed to do. Occasionally Brad would stroke Storm's hair or shoulder, giving Storm permission to lean closer against him as a cat, dog or small child would do with one who was loved and trusted.

When Storm was at last secured to the wall, blindfolded, tit clamps attached to his nipples and a weight attached to his balls, his manhood was at once tumescent, dripping the honey of love. What was to take place, he wondered? What would happen tonight that would give Sir cause to be proud of his boy? He wondered but felt no fear.

The soft thud of a leather flogger warmed his back and limbs, then the belt, then another flogger, this one harder and stiffer than the first. Storm writhed against the restraints but kept his body presented toward Sir, knowing as he did from his reading the fearsome punishments that met a boy who pulled away from his Master's lash. His body danced in space, his voice cried out in joy, oblivious to the lash, the crop, the belt. Then Sir was standing in front of him, kissing him, holding him, whispering encouragement for what was to come.

"Listen, baby boy, Daddy has a surprise for you."

"Sir?"

"A buddy of mine is here with a single tail. Do you know what that is, boy?"

"Yes, Sir. I read about them."

"Of course you did, boy. My buddy is going to use the single tail on you while I hold you. Do you trust Daddy?"

"Yes, Sir."

Brad nodded, Storm knew though he couldn't see Sir, and the lash cracked in the air and kissed Storm's back, breaking the skin and drawing blood. Storm screamed.

"Good boy, you can take it."

"Yes, Sir," he whimpered.

The lash cracked the air again, and a second welt as bloody as the first was painted across the flesh. Then a third lash, a fourth and fifth. Then it ended. Storm's knees buckled but he was caught by Sir, who held him up as others released him, removed tit clamps and ball weight, provoking a vague agony that Storm hardly noticed. The man with the single tail helped Brad carry Storm to the couch. Ice was applied to the wounds, then salve, and then a clean white T-shirt. Storm came to, happy to be the subject of such tender ministrations. He opened his eyes to see Sir's proud but anxious face. Storm was going to apologize for collapsing, for not lasting through the ten lashes that he had promised himself to endure.

Instead he said, "I love you, Sir."

"I love you, boy."

The hard leather collar was removed, and a lighter, silver one was locked around Storm's neck. Storm touched the lock and smiled.

* * *

A year later, Sir took Storm to San Francisco for Folsom Weekend. Storm walked through the Fair naked except for boots, the leather shorts, the silver collar and the thicker leather collar, added for the occasion, as it sometimes was, to accommodate the leash. Having been flogged the night before, he proudly displayed the welts covering his body. He was just as proud of the proper beard Sir had allowed him to grow, and he felt more wholly male than he had at any time in his life.

"Here, boy," said Sir putting some bills in Storm's hand and tucking the end of the leash in Storm's back pocket. "Get us some beers."

"Yes, Sir."

Storm was happier at that moment than he could recall being since the silver chain was locked around his neck, never to be removed. He waited patiently in line, graciously accepting the admiration of some, oblivious to the envy of boys without Sirs. He was heading back with the beers when a familiar voice called his name. He turned: it was Dale.

"Storm?"

Dale looked good, as he always did, shirtless and sweetly furry, leather jeans clinging tightly to his legs and buttocks.

"Dale."

"Baby, what happened to you?"

"Happened?"

"I mean, you ran out on me like that."

"No, you ran out on me, as I recall."

"But, baby, I was coming back. I didn't know you'd left until a couple months later when I came by looking for you."

Storm smirked, imagining Dale's consternation on discovering the notice to vacate on the door of the apartment. *Sweet,* he thought.

"And what's this, baby?" Dale asked tugging on the dog collar and leash.

"What it looks like."

"Did I drive you to this? Baby, I'd never treat you like that."

"No, you wouldn't. So it's good you dumped me, so I could find the man who does."

Storm almost skipped back to Sir.

"Who were you talking to, boy?"

"My last and worst boyfriend, Sir, the one who left me all that leather porn."

"So I have him to thank?"

"No, Sir. I'm all my own doing, except for that part of me that you uncovered, Sir."

Sir lifted his beer into the air in a toast and Storm followed his example, clicking the flimsy plastic cups and spilling beer onto the dirty pavement, some of it landing on Sir's boot. Without a word, Storm knelt and licked the boot clean. Sir laughed with pride.

"That'll do, pig."

JIMMY TEMPLE

David Ciminello

Jimmy Temple explains how to fuck a girl. "Girls have dicks," he says.

"No they don't."

"Oh, yes they do. I have sisters. And they all have dicks. They're small. But they're there."

Jimmy is taller than the baby pines around Packanack Lake. His wrists seem as thick as their trunks. His fingers are long, the nails square. He always holds his cigarette between his thumb and forefinger. Until he flicks it into the dirt.

"A girl's cunt can comfortably hold something the width of a baseball bat," he says. "So, I'm okay."

His smile is all white. A neat row of Chiclets.

"The first girl I ever pumped was Ginny Moscher. Sweet," he says. "Her insides tasted like lemon saltwater taffy and baked clams with melted butter."

* * *

At home the refrigerator clicks and buzzes recharging itself. The kitchen rattles with it. The fake brick linoleum hums clean, freshly waxed. It squeaks from my shoes. There is no dinner on the stove. No warmth comes from the oven. Only the scent of my mother's depression enters the room—a greeting from upstairs.

She is in bed again, the door closed. Life exhausts her. It was all she could do to mop the floor.

I knock on the door. "You awake?"

In the George Washington Middle School cafeteria they pump a pop station in over the announcement system. This and the chocolate milkshakes work to calm the monsters. Treats to a den of lions.

Jimmy Temple has been expelled from school three times. The third time is two weeks before Halloween.

"I'm not going trick-or-treating this year," he says. "No one is. They made it illegal."

"No, they haven't."

"Oh, yes they have. It was in all the papers."

"Since when do you read the papers?"

"Since I started goddamned current events in social studies."

The house I live in is big. When it storms the plate glass window in the formal living room rattles from the thunder. During hurricane season the tall oaks in the neighbor's backyard bend all the way to the ground and kiss the grass.

"How was school today?" she says.

"Fine."

The table is set for four. There is stew on the stove. Bread in the oven. An iceberg salad with quartered tomatoes and sliced cucumbers dressed with fake French dressing (really whipped mayo and ketchup) on the counter. She is in the same housecoat and sweater.

"Did you go to the library after school?"

"Yes."

"Do you want rice with your stew, or noodles?"

"Noodles."

Always noodles.

"A sure thing," Jimmy says. "I'm a sure thing kind of guy." The pat on my head feels like a validation. More than the constant stream of dinner noodles.

"Ever wonder how they get the eggs in those tiny little noodles?" Jimmy laughs. The clubhouse-sized cement pipe we inhabit at the bottom of the pipeline is cool in the May heat. The constant hissing and clicks of the cicadas echo inside. The crack-riddled pipe can fit four people. Easy.

"I hate bugs," Jimmy says. He snaps his Day-Glo orange ("*Dago* orange," he calls it) Bic lighter on and fries an ant. It pops and sizzles. A small spurt of smoke flares up. Dead-bug smell fills the pipe.

Jimmy Temple never goes to the library. "What do I need a library for?" While walking down Seneca Trail, he flicks another cigarette to the ground. "Boring," he says. His T-shirt is yellow, the color of the buttercups that sprout on Mr. Rome's lawn. The sun is brighter. The pavement vibrates. He picks an empty Tab can off the strip of dry grass between the sidewalk and street and twists it in half, scraping the knuckles on his hands. Small pinpoints of blood erupt.

"How was school today?" he asks in a mocking tone.

"Mr. Rodgers caught Bruce Goldbloom and I cutting gym again."

"Bruce and me," he says.

"What?"

"Only assholes get caught."

She skirts through the house thinking about her two sons and her husband, the dentist. She sits on her end of the couch and lights another Viceroy. The blinds are down, blocking out Wayne, New Jersey. She thinks about Massachusetts. Takes an even pull off the cancer stick and lets her mind wander through the apple orchards of Taunton. There the sun is on her legs (the legs her own mother wouldn't let her shave when she was a puberty-riddled girl). This is how she spends her afternoons now. Her mornings. Her days. Alone in this split-level ranch in Wayne floating to other places.

We are back in the giant pipe. Another hot summer day. Jimmy burns another bug. The sun edges in.

"Take off your shirt," he says.

The humidity feels like the locker room at the school gym after the showers run for a while. I'm all clammy skin and lazy limbs.

Jimmy smiles.

The cracks in the pipe multiply.

Dinner can be a platter of breaded veal cutlets (fried in the big Farberware frying pan). Green beans in a big milk glass bowl, butter pats already melted. This night a tall bottle of Brook-dale grape soda stands in the center of the table. Glasses loaded with ice clink-melt at the tops of the empty dinner plates. It is Wednesday. She lights another Viceroy and offers mashed potatoes. The night is cool so the air-conditioning is off. The phone rings.

"Hello, Mother," she says.

It is Grandma.

"Just myself and the boys," she says into the phone. A suck off her cigarette then a long slow exhale.

Grandma's squawk jumps out of the phone.

"Veal cutlets," my mother says.

"*Squawk, squawk*," goes the phone.

My mother responds, "And mashed potatoes."

"*Squawk? Squawk?*"

"Yes, I'll have enough for Sunday." She rolls her eyes and travels back to the apple orchards in Taunton.

My bedroom walls are papered with dead grass. The sheets on my bed are always clean. It is late evening. Sounds from across the street slip through the screen above my desk. A weak breeze burps loose notebook pages along the blotter. Across the street the Morelli boys crack bottles against their curb (Kurt, Scott, Tony—wannabe rebels without a cause). The pungent odor of pot fingers its way into my room. My sheets are cool. The specter of Jimmy Temple hovers over my bed. He fills the night sky of my ceiling and smiles.

"How was school today?"

"Fine."

"Take off your shirt."

In her room, she lies next to my father. He snorts in his sleep. She lights another cigarette. The tip flares in the cocoon of her cave. Momma Bear with Papa Bear. She glances at Papa's lumpy silhouette. The wrinkled clump of blanket rises and falls. She knows he is filling teeth in his dreams. Drilling and telling people to spit.

* * *

"You ever do drugs?" Jimmy tightens the laces on his Converse high-tops. Only one week left of summer. The giant pipe is cooler than usual.

"I tried pot once."

"Liar."

He digs into his front pocket, reaches down to the very bottom. His hand comes out. Two little pills dot the space between his pinky and thumb.

"One for you and one for me," he says. "Bottoms up."

My mother is alone in our house, smoking and watching television. She travels back to Massachusetts and feels the wet grass between her toes. (Another suck off her cigarette.) Her Aunt Olive is teaching her to crochet. Ribs bake in Auntie's oven. The barbecue sauce–saturated meat falls off the bones. The blanket my mother works on barely covers her lap.

"It will get bigger," Aunt Olive says. "Don't fret, Shirley," she says. "You'll get there."

Back in Wayne the old blanket is over her legs. It almost covers the whole bed, each stitch a monument to her dead aunt. She nubs her cigarette (crushes it in the ashtray on the nightstand), fingers the pilled wool, and lights another.

In the pipe I imagine Jimmy Temple's house smells like hunger. His mother works two jobs. Dinner might be Wonder Bread and Oscar Meyer with Hellmann's. The floor of the pipe feels like the inside of a refrigerator. Hard and cold. Jimmy breathes heavily. His breath is fire. The pills make the pipe rotate (like the entrance to the Freakytown Funhouse in Seaside Heights). Belts are unbuckled. Zippers unzipped. (Jimmy uses his teeth.)

He tastes like Palmolive Soap and salt. There is so much

there. Very thick. (It *is* like the bottom of a baseball bat!) The ridge fans around. The shaft is hard. He smells like the old baby blanket tucked in the top of the toy closet back home on Harrison Road. There is enough to choke on without going all the way down. But Jimmy won't let me stop.

TRUNK

Trebor Healey

E nding up in the trunk of a car headed for Houston was not what Bobby'd had in mind when he came to New Orleans. Of course, he hadn't counted on vomiting on the shoes of the Reverend Norman DuMay either, nor running into the likes of Old Croc and his creepy mojo medicine. In fact, Bobby'd come to New Orleans in order to avoid such things (an ironically interesting choice for such an escape), to lay low and get his life in order, to do the right thing. He'd come to volunteer, to help rebuild in the aftermath of Katrina, to turn over a new leaf for himself and his relationship to the world.

That's what he told himself, anyway.

On a more visceral level, he'd been drawn like a magnet to the Crescent City out of an odd sort of identification. He wasn't so much appalled and horrified by Katrina as he was pruriently and subliminally intrigued with it. Perhaps it was a conviction that he was sinking fast and that what was happening on the flooded streets of New Orleans was a disturbingly apt metaphor for his own inundation—with booze, semen, crystal meth, and all manner of unbridled desire. What was that old line of Hamlet's? "'Tis better to take arms against a sea of troubles, and by opposing, end them?" Maybe he and this dear unfortunate city could help each other? Something like that. Bobby wasn't thinking too clearly. New Orleans as Yorick? Or was it all a fool's errand? Call it a sort of megalomaniacal codependence; call it a cry for a help; call it a cautionary tale for the neocon dream or any other twisted sort of messianic hogwash. Bobby was looking for an anchor, and what better place to look for it than the sea.

Glued as he'd been to his television set and his laptop through most of September, he'd witnessed the National Guard in their speedboats rescuing dogs and obese women off roofs; he'd seen the Superdome packed to bursting, the president smugly attempting a riff on "ich bin ein New Orleanian," though it came out "moron" or "asshole"—Bobby couldn't tell which. Neither he nor the leader of the free world could speak French.

Eight months later, channel surfing the TV, his laptop balanced on his knees, Bobby once again blazed to the nines on speed, with no fewer than nine IM boxes open with such names as 9inchbliss, Gutterthroat, and Gettheebehindmesatan, it dawned on him that no one was really doing anything much about the fate of New Orleans—least of all him (he'd been too broke buying drugs and booze to even send the meager twenty-five dollars in response to that letter from the Red Cross that came with the return address labels he'd been using for the past year)—and that no one likely would. It had become a lousy reality TV show with no plot other than "the government doesn't care, it really doesn't." Katrina gave sink or swim a whole new meaning. Laissez-faire. Well, it was a French term and New Orleans was the Frenchest of cities, and America hates the French—even begrudges them their fries

now that the holy war is on. Meanwhile the vice president bela-
bors the country with the intricacies of flood insurance fraud
when he's not shooting his friends in the face with buckshot, and
the president is too busy feeding Christmas trees into a shredder
(wait those aren't trees, they're young men!) to be bothered with
such inconsequential things as chocolate cities—though he did
call his white friend "Brownie." Hey, let 'em eat brownies. But
who was George Bush, anyway—Willy Wonka? Did he look like
Johnny Depp? No. He was a godly man; he had people to kill
and nations to destroy. The Lord's work. He'd as likely rebuild
New Orleans as he would Iraq or the Tower of Babel.

Bobby snorted another line, muttering, "Man, this country
sucks."

Moments later, he nearly choked as he quaffed another Sierra
Nevada. Sink or swim. A jolt of guilt shook him, and he looked
around the room—clothes strewn about, scattered empty beer
bottles, and tiny cans of amyl nitrate; fast-food bags and wrappers; a hole where his friend Kip had punctured the drywall
during a particularly out-of-hand sex scene. What on earth was
going on? How many beers had he drained while watching the
news reports of the devastation over those past nine months?
How many porn sites and Internet chat rooms had he barreled
into, ignoring the news stories of Katrina's wrath and aftermath
on the portal pages on his way in and out, while the tragedy
droned on at low volume from the TV across the room? How
many lines of speed had he snorted, brilliant white as a Katrina
trailer? How many boys had flooded him? Had he flooded?
All while the levees sat unrepaired. How many times had his
heart filled with horror and repulsion that he was comparing his
pathetic broken-down life—albeit one with a roof over his head,
a job, and three squares—to victims of a natural disaster? Was
his life really an ongoing hurricane? Was it that bad? Was he

that self-indulgent? He looked in the mirror, chipped the crusted scab of a speed bump off his cheek. Even FEMA wouldn't be able to help *him*. It was that bad. A line from back in the day when gay people had a political conscience flitted through his mind: the personal is political.

He thought of Father Robert, his Jesuit uncle. What had he always said? If things are really bad, and beyond help, go help someone else. Of course, that was easy for him to say. He had a vocation. What did Bobby have? A big dick? An AA degree? A habit?

There were lists of organizations on the *L.A. Times* website. He steered clear of the Christians, as he knew from experience that he'd always end up on the wrong end of a Bible quote with those geeks. He was a proud, out homo and that wasn't something he was willing to put aside. This was about helping other people, not sucking it up and taking abuse from selfish fucks whose only motivation was their own sanctimony and a low-point mortgage in the afterlife.

There was the Red Cross, the United Way, etc., but he didn't want to end up in some office in Baton Rouge. He wanted to be on the ground, knee-deep in it, just like he was in his own self-destruction. He chanced upon something called GUMBO (Greater United Metropolitan Betterment Organization), which looked sufficiently lefty and irreverent to be prohomo or at least laissez-faire about such things (one picture of its volunteers had a group of dreadlocked hippie boys playing Hacky Sack in a park, while nearby little girls in cornrows played ring-around-the-rosy). No-brainer. He immediately filled out the volunteer application form to join a crew gutting damaged houses for poor folks with no insurance in the Ninth Ward.

The minute he clicked to submit his application, he was ecstatic and felt newly self-empowered. He began cleaning up his room, the poppers and beer cans clanging together like the opening bars to some cheesy musical: *Poppers and beer cans and sweet apple strudel, faggots and rainbows and...* He felt—well—good, upbeat, upstanding, well-endowed, and attractive; a sure bet to get laid. He was full of himself, a narcissistic federal disaster area that Mr. Bush would be wise to do absolutely nothing for. *I'm an activist*, Bobby congratulated himself; *a do-gooder; part of the solution; a relief worker.* He felt so good, he threw a going-away party for himself, got shit-faced drunk, and blew his friend Ed in the bathroom.

Of course, what Bobby found in New Orleans was anything but relief.

It started on the airplane, where a comely flight attendant named Bo scribbled his hotel room number on a cocktail napkin after shamelessly flirting and feeding Bobby free gin and tonics between Phoenix and New Orleans.

Bobby made it a point to stop at three cocktails and took no speed breaks in the bathroom, telling himself he would simply make it a date and not do anything sexual.

He failed.

But he only had one bump, two beers, and he used a condom. Progress. And at least it gave him a place to sleep his first night in New Orleans.

He set out early next morning as the steward had an eight a.m. flight to Minneapolis and was clearly moving on to the next thing, showering and chattering on his cell phone while Bobby gathered his things together like a hobo, more or less ignored by his host.

He got a quick insincere smile and a small wave as the glorified waitress chortled on about the Denver-to-Dallas route with some queeny colleague, slamming the door behind Bobby as if he were putting the dog out, his gaze all but averted. In fact,

Bobby barked, assuming of course that the joke would go unnoticed, as it did to all but himself.

He stumbled onto the streets of Metairie, which didn't look half bad, considering what had happened a year prior. He'd expected worse. He hailed a cab for downtown so he could stroll through the beloved historic district and assess the damage on his way to the GUMBO office out past the Marigny in the Gentilly District. He wanted to wallow in his heroism a bit, which was markedly different from what he usually wallowed in when he visited New Orleans for Southern Decadence each year. He purposely avoided Bourbon Street, strolling along Royal Street at first and then cutting up to Burgundy, threading his way around the "trouble spots" that might derail his "new leaf."

To his surprise, the French Quarter looked downright passable—in fact, he wouldn't have known there was a hurricane if he hadn't looked for the broken windows and damaged, tarped roofs, which were incidentally loaded with hot-looking Latin boys, hammering about and being masculine. Thank God they had work to do or he might have lingered.

Then things quickly deteriorated as Bobby headed out into the neighborhoods. Enormous trees upended, piles of refuse up and down the curbs, Katrina trailers parked here and there asserting their ugliness while the charming houses desolately frowned with abandonment, shamed at their high-water marks and concave porches like week-old diapers no one had bothered to change.

He checked in at the GUMBO office on Elysian Fields, a fairly undamaged area, if you ignored the blue tarps draped across every other roof, the boarded-up windows, and the ubiquitous red spray paint graffitied on every other house with dates and numerical renderings of how many dogs or people were left inside in need of rescue or food drops.

He thought briefly of Noah—his ex, not the biblical character. Noah had been a contractor. He'd also gone off the deep end with speed and vanished into the digital divide—he was either addicted to porn and Internet cruising or unable to pay his ISP bill, Bobby could never remember which. Regardless, the results were more or less the same. Man overboard.

The folks at GUMBO were smart, informed, and not fucking around. "We're here because the government isn't, and we aren't surprised about that." Bobby felt that old dread of self-righteous lesbianism that every circuit fool gayboy feels when his Peter Pandom is exposed under the glaring lights of women who have moved beyond taking care of and making excuses for boys.

"Uh, yeah, great... Uh, me, too," he fumbled.

"Well, welcome Robert," the pretty mulatto girl answered.

"Call me Bobby?"

She gave a quick smile, as if he'd cracked a bad joke, and reached into a drawer for some materials he'd need to read.

His first order of business was to get settled in a house GUMBO'd recently set up for them. He and eight other volunteers would bunk there while he completed his three-week volunteer gig.

It was only a few blocks away, so he hoofed it over there, and sure enough it was rife with hippie boys in various states of undress. New Orleans is hot and humid, not a place for clothing. But the thrill soon paled after he listened to them talk for a bit. Hopelessly straight and conventional and moralistic, like most hippie boys, Bobby was soon annoyed by their unavailable prettiness, their reggae music, their guitars and bongo drums. He knew he'd likely be keeping more or less to himself, and that none of these boys would likely give it up for the visiting fag, no matter how hip and cool they thought themselves. "Yo bra, nice dreadlocks, chocolate city, yeah," and the ghetto fist-play greeting.

He grabbed an empty bunk in the last room down the hall and headed to the bathroom, where he deposited what proved to be a traveler's turd, challenging the plumbing with its size and girth. As the water swirled and rose, Bobby felt a sudden shame, thinking that what New Orleans, of all cities, really didn't need was another turd floating down the street. He felt guilty, Californian, a fuckup, a bad omen; he panicked. He searched the bathroom for a plunger. He flushed again. The toilet water rose on his own private Katrina moment, nearly cresting the rim before it began to retreat. *Thank God porcelain has integrity,* he thought as the water ebbed.

He went for help.

"No problem, dude, we all get traveler's turd on the road. There's a plunger on the back porch." Sheesh, what a frat house. He went to work with it, and as he plunged the third time, the plunger turned inside out, and then quickly inverted itself, splattering shit across the walls, the toilet, and all over the front of Bobby's clothing. *Welcome to chocolate city,* he thought in disgust. An omen indeed. And then he heard the toilet drain, cough, and swallow. Praise Jesus.

Back at the GUMBO office, showered and decked out in cargo shorts and a polo shirt, Bobby mustered up the best attitude he could. The place was a zoo, and orientation was haphazard and fast. He was issued a white safety suit, as the dangers of toxic poisoning were substantial. He hadn't bargained for that. He'd heard of mold allergies and figured they couldn't kill him, but exposure to asbestos? Because what GUMBO did was gut and dismantle houses—something not covered by most insurance (and who had flood insurance anyway? Who could afford it?). And with a price tag of 7K, GUMBO was forced to beg donations and volunteers in order to make a dent in what was otherwise an almost insurmountable expense for most people.

Admirably and against all odds, thanks to donations, sheer will, and an adopt-a-house program, they were getting people back into their homes, albeit slowly.

Bobby rushed home and modeled the white suit. It was made out of that weird sort of part plastic, part paper, part foil, part cloth stuff. The mask looked sexy at least—dangerous, scifi authoritarian—and like baggy jeans on a boy, the suit hung slack at the crotch and ass, so that if you could get beyond its clownish appearance, your imagination could conjure up tight butts and low-hanging balls, big uncut schlongs swinging pendulous and unimpeded like censers in search of a sanctuary. "My body is a temple," Bobby muttered. And he thought of Jared, Lars, Dylan, Josh, and Bennett in the next room, and how loose and naked their bodies floated inside those suits, like astronauts in space, the thick foliage where the hair stood out above their oversized cocks, like a fecund flower box on some resurrected shotgun shack of New Orleans. Bobby's fantasy soon tented the gossamer fibers of the suit's fabric—and it wouldn't be the last time—forcing him in the days following to repeatedly pretend that he needed to squat down to get at low chunks of insulation still clinging or scattered along the bottom of dismantled walls.

On one such occasion, the reverend showed up.

"I swear you look like children of the Rapture in those white suits. And so you are! Heh, heh. What you doing down there, son?"

Busted. Bobby looked up over his shoulder from his crouched position. "Uh, just doing what I came here to do, sir. To make these houses habitable again."

"Just in time for the next storm," the Reverend DuMay chuckled, ducking under a scaffold and making his way through the little shotgun house Bobby had been assigned to work on his first week along with a one-week veteran, Tony, a Catholic boy from Boston—definitely not one of the hippie boys. Bobby did a double take on the reverend as he moved on.

"How you doin', son, welcome to God's country," DuMay beamed, greeting Tony.

Bobby stared, rapt. He'd never met a Southern preacher before.

"Has the Lord reached you, son, or are you lost still?" A grin crossed DuMay's face, and Bobby's jaw went slack as he awaited Tony's reply.

Tony didn't miss a beat. "Jesus is my Lord and savior, sir." And they high-fived. So much for avoiding Christians.

The reverend guffawed. "Oh, son, you are ripe. Ripe as a swollen peach. I could just pick you off the tree." And he laughed and pinched Tony's cheek as if he were a small child. Then he turned and winked at Bobby, before walking out the back and on to the next house.

"Who is *that*?" Bobby asked Tony, incredulous.

"Oh, that's the reverend. He's harmless."

"As in the crazy being harmless?"

"Oh, he's into Armageddon." And he shrugged his shoulders. "Takes all kinds."

Bobby scrunched his eyes. "Does it?"

"God works in strange ways. I mean all the reverend asks is if you've accepted Jesus Christ? Haven't you?"

"Sure, what the fuck, he's welcome along with everyone else. I don't play favorites."

"He's the only one."

Bobby glared at him. "Aren't you a *Catholic*?"

"Yeah," he said defensively, "we believe in Jesus, too."

Bobby arched his brows, but couldn't help smiling. Born of a long line of Marian heretics, Bobby thought it a dubious argument at best. But wasn't it just his luck that he got paired up with the religious one out of all the cute little humanist hippies, who were probably Wiccans or Buddhists. Then again, his chances of sex were probably higher with Tony, as a good fifty percent of Christian boys were major fence-sitters. *It's a fuckin' gay religion,* he thought, and he meant *gay* like a twelve-year-old meant it.

But Tony was kind of cute. In fact, he had a twinkle in his eye that Bobby was beginning to think was not the Holy Spirit. There's only one other kind of man who has such a twinkle in his eye. Well, twinkle or no, Tony also had a fat, homely fiancée named Emily whose picture was tucked in the frame of the Anglo Jesus portrait above his bed, right next to the palm frond from Palm Sunday. Damning evidence. Bobby saw him as several years shy of the self-discovery and reflection necessary to go down on a guy, but he also suspected that in time he would. Bobby didn't have that kind of time, and certainly didn't have that kind of patience—but then again, shouldn't he at least try to move things along for Emily's sake?

Lust springs eternal.

But how? He'd committed to three weeks. Oh, sure, one part of Bobby thought that was plenty of time. An hour was enough with a lot of men. But he'd need privacy and some downtime, a little booze—none of which were abundant, if available at all, in the bunkhouses of GUMBO.

They went back to work, lugging a stove out to the curb, hacking up some water-damaged furniture, and chipping away at more of the walls and ceilings. Quitting time came and they went out front to survey the Katrina pile they'd made, which they proudly compared to the other less towering ones up and down the street.

They unzipped their suits, and climbed out of them.

"Damn, it's hot," Tony whined, stripping off his T-shirt to

reveal his excruciatingly perfect little chest. Ouch. Elvis Presley's "Don't Be Cruel" lullabyed through Bobby's code-red-alerted brain. Good God, but lust was merciless. And never one to pass up even a semblance of opportunity—or failing that, just some good old-fashioned interactive homoeroticism—Bobby did the same. They looked at each other. "Dude, you're ripped," Tony shared.

"You, too, man. You work out?"

"Nah, just lucky I guess."

"Lucky, eh?" *No, it's Emily who's lucky,* Bobby thought. Tony, he was about to go home and step in a pile of karmic shit called marriage that was far more substantial than any Katrina pile.

Just then the reverend came strolling by on his way back to wherever he came from before his visit. "Better keep those suits on, boys; the Lord comes like a thief in the night. Heh, heh, heh. Wouldn't wanna miss him." And he waved and hopped into a chauffeured blue Crown Victoria parked two doors down.

"Can't they like get a restraining order for that guy?" Bobby thoughtlessly said into the middle distance.

Tony furrowed his brow. "It's a free country, dude. Jesus rocks." Bobby just looked at him and nodded slowly.

Unlike Tony and Bobby, the reverend wasn't part of GUMBO, though he took it upon himself to inspect their work often and "minister to them," as he called it. He ran his own outfit called BIO, which stood for "Bring It On," meaning the apocalypse. He was sure it was coming and thought the rebuilding effort foolish. But he was doing a lot of good in his own fashion, through his soup kitchens and revival flea markets where people could barter all manner of goods, and the faithful could come down from Kansas or Missouri and do big giveaways with whatever they had to offer: clothes mostly, canned goods, soap.

No, sir, he didn't see Katrina the same way the lefties did. He was elated with the nearness of Armageddon and thought GUMBO a bunch of ignorant, godless liberals, suffering under the sin of pride, thinking they could avert the wrath of God, offering false promise and material assistance to poor wayward lambs. He'd sort of stroll around the GUMBO houses, shaking hands, clearly struggling with his own pride issues, a gaggle of sycophants at his heels. Tacky as Jim Jones, he had a thick white mane of hair and wore purple-tinted oversized aviator glasses and beige leisure suits that swelled with his girth and shook when he laughed. "You're not that different from a bunch of communists really—and we know where they ended." And he'd burst out laughing. At times like that, Bobby wanted to snap back, "Yeah, well you ain't that different than Il Duce or Herman Goering, and they ended worse."

It was good he didn't though, because everyone laughed along with the reverend, and in fact, liked him. He had charisma, and a ready smile, a Southern congeniality that made him basi-cally un-hateable. Besides, some of the hippie boys were in fact *wearing* Che shirts, and the word on the street was the levees were in no shape to hold back another Katrina, which would once again flood every single house GUMBO was repairing. So the reverend had a point, whether you wanted to reflect on it or not, or whether you espoused his biblical paradigm. And on top of all that, as everyone at GUMBO knew, the man had been there from the start feeding and sheltering people in tents, and his credibility in terms of relief work was unquestioned. On some level, they were all in it together, and he was just betting on a different horse than they were. The differences between GUMBO and the Reverend DuMay was along the lines of the friendly banter between White Sox and Cubs fans, although with far more dire consequences for the winners and losers.

But couldn't the reverend put a cork in it? The hippie boys weren't proselytizing about Buddha or Leonard Peltier, after all. But DuMay just chattered on endlessly, full of the confident bludgeoning rhetoric of an unquestionably dominant religion, while he meandered about the houses, his booming voice echoing off what was the left of the walls. "The president loves New Orleans, like he loves Jesus. We're the chosen people, and the president is proud of our witnessing. There's no city he cares for more. Why we're like the troops. In harm's way— no holier place to be. The president knows that; he supports us as God supports the righteous. He's in awe of the grace of our crucifixion, and when the great hurricane Lucifer Katrina the Second comes, he knows we will be lifted up like buoys. Oh, ye of little faith, ye liberal devils, trying to drown us in your thirty pieces of silver. No, Lord, we don't want this cup to pass. We want to drink it down, drown in your righteousness. You oughta all go home and get your own houses in order, not ours."

"But, but…" Tony attempted a response. When conservative and liberal Christians collide.

"But nothing, son," and he guffawed.

Stern words, but the smile always spread across his face whenever he was most scolding, in effect emasculating and charming every audience that heard him. He was a preacher all right, the likes of which Bobby'd never seen. After all, Bobby had been raised Catholic, and Catholic priests were generally either white liberal wimps, corny yarn-spinning Irishmen, or besotted unimaginative English majors who churned out bad critical essays in place of sermons, outlining why the resurrection made things different than if he hadn't been resurrected, or why it's better to obey your mom than to tell her to fuck off. No duh. So Bobby had slept a lot during mass, when he wasn't fantasizing about the altar boys or other parishioners while the priest droned on.

But he listened when the reverend spoke. How he listened. The Reverend DuMay was an artist of the first order. He left people speechless, and Bobby found himself drawn to him.

"How you doing, Mr. Kennedy...Mr. Attorney General of thee You-nited States," he'd joke, "did you catch all the Mafiosi yet?! Heh, heh, heh. Mark my words, son, they'll shoot a proud man before they'll give him the keys to heaven. George Bush is a righteous man. It's written in the stars." And he'd gesture with his hand toward the sky.

Bobby would just laugh back, but he could detect the subtext, though he resisted the temptation to deconstruct the reverend's balderdash to preserve his own peace of mind. What was the point with these people? When all was said and done, Bobby found it simpler to just treat the reverend like a very good stand-up comic who he didn't always agree with, but who, he had to admit, was very entertaining. A guilty pleasure. He wondered if the reverend was aware that many people probably saw him this way—as a sort of clown. Bobby thought he was, and as if he were reading his mind, the reverend soon enough eerily quipped, "I'm but a fool, Bobby, an instrument. Oh, His glory is great." And he smiled ear to ear.

An answer for everything.

Well, try this on for size, Reverend. Bobby was jonesing for speed, and though he'd on several occasions shared a beer or two with the boys back at the house, in between Hacky Sack sessions, he was determined not to fall back into drunkenness and debauchery, sex in alleys, and most of all the ever-destructive crystal. He'd fought the good fight for two weeks. A new leaf. God, but he was horny as sin, and he'd fought too hard to be queer and proud to classify good sex as depraved along the lines of alcohol and speed. He'd vowed to have only healthy sex. But how does one find good, healthy sex? He didn't have the patience, and what's more, GUMBO was straight as the siding on a Katrina trailer. He was over outreach fantasies for the hippies, and Tony…oh, Tony. Tony was ruining him with desire. Lately, Tony had developed an annoying habit of looking over from his ladder like a bro and smiling. Bobby had tolerated it at first, when he was still busy collecting the requisite masturbation material for later, like a bird feathering its nest. But after a week, every smile felt like Eros pulling back his bow: One, two, three—all day long like Bobby was a hay bale or a sitting duck. He felt swollen and tenderized, sensitive to any touch. Tony just kept smiling and firing away, the heartless bastard. And then of course, there was the "Jesus rocks" answer to any and all good news or commonsense truth shared with him—the Christian rocker's amen.

"Nice day."

"Jesus rocks."

"I like these crowbars."

"Jesus rocks."

And the hugs. Oh, the hugs. "Blessings, dude." At the end of every workday. But never when they'd taken their shirts off. Oh, no. Always once they'd put them back on. The cheap bastard. Bobby soon took to scowling at Tony's smiles and dodging his hugs. He knew it wasn't nice, but he couldn't stand the tease of it, even if Tony would never conceive of it as such. Tony was an idiot and a vacuous phony. But a hot one.

Tony eventually got the hint that Bobby wasn't into Jesus or his smiles—or was it more like he'd begun to feel that there was chemistry between them? That's when he'd start going on and on about his wedding to Emily, planned for when he got back to Boston.

"How old are you, Tony?"

"Twenty," he defensively answered.

"Isn't that kind of young to be getting married?"

"Better to marry than to burn."

I prefer fire, Bobby thought to say as a luscious bead of sweat rolled down Tony's cheek and onto his smiling upper lip. As Bobby gazed at the beautiful boy, their eyes locked in platonic love—or something—he knew what that night would bring. He'd had it. *Hell or high water.* Yeah, exactly. The water had receded, so he knew what part of that cliché was heading his way.

He'd stayed away for two weeks, but now he was dead set on Bourbon Street and the notorious Corner Pocket, where the dregs of the parish stripped for change, and the beer and speed breached the levee of whatever inhibitions remained in the poor lost lambs of the French Quarter.

It was Tony's fault, not his.

Tony did his bare-chested routine as usual at the end of the day, and this time Bobby just stared, quickly slurping up the drool that threatened to fall from his lower lip. Tony said, "What, dude?"

Bobby just shook his head. Tonight he'd clear the slate. He'd go down to Bourbon Street and clear the slate. He'd held out long enough. He'd avoided drunkenness, drugs, sex, and even fallen for a clean-living Christian and done the Lord's work. *But God, I miss that old leaf,* he sighed.

"You wanna go out tonight? Like down to Bourbon Street?" Bobby chanced.

"No."

"Great. See you tomorrow."

On went the shirt. "Blessings." The embrace. A stirring in Bobby's crotch. They parted and Bobby waved, and it was all he could do to keep the digits surrounding his middle finger from dropping into a little fist.

Bobby didn't bother going home for a shower. He knew he looked enticingly blue-collar and was in no mood for anyone looking for a clean-cut soap-smelling boy anyway. He was looking for another beast.

He marched down Elysian Fields, sweat cresting his brow, the humidity so thick the clouds and the sky sort of merged into an amorphous bluish white-gray steam. He cut up Frenchmen, and, crossing Esplanade—one signal-light post stuck like a tiki torch in the grass at a forty-five degree angle (ah, the charms and grandeur of hurricanian ruination)—he had a laugh and thought of the River Styx. Whatever Eurydice he sought would be a sorry wreck of a slut indeed.

Sylvester was crooning at top volume when he entered the Bourbon Pub, and eyes swung about from the surrounding men as he entered from the street: some like babies toward shiny things, a handful like prowling cats, and still others like roused guard dogs who wanted a piece of his flesh or at least a good chase and tackle before moving on.

He glared back with his usual fuck-you-all visage, acquired among the clubs of L.A., and approached the bar. A sorry-looking go-go boy gyrated in a pair of boxer briefs, and Bobby momentarily wished the lad's pecs were as full of air as they looked so he could prick one with a pin and watch the boy fly around the room like a deflating balloon.

That's when he felt a distinctly reptilian presence at his side. He quickly glanced over out of a sort of animal watchfulness, and who did he see sitting on the stool next to him at the bar but the Reverend DuMay himself, a pack of Marlboros and a cocktail perched in front of him, like some flaming queen, his hair coiffed, and sporting a big oversized yellow-print Hawaiian shirt. He, too, looked at Bobby with the eyes of a hunter, but more like one with a long tongue that would strangle you in its embrace. Then he grinned, erasing all threat.

Figures the reverend would be queer. Bobby felt so tired suddenly.

"It's Saturday night, son, and the Sabbath is just around the corner. What are you doing in this den of iniquity?"

"Oh, just a little R&R, Father." Bobby was in no mood. He felt like he'd crossed over at Esplanade and was through with the provincial squeamishness of do-gooders and hypocritical Christians alike.

"I'm not a Father, son, I'm a reverend."

"Oh, sorry, I was raised Catholic."

"I suspected as much; you've always had the stink of popery about ya."

He clipped a quick smile. "And what exactly kind of stink is that, Reverend?" he shot back.

"Sorta like sulfur, like frankincense and myrrh, but cooked a spell too long. Heh, heh, heh." And then, "Can I buy you a drink, son?"

"Sure. Bud Light. Thanks." Why not use the reverend to get the buzz going, he figured.

"One Bud Light and one seven-and-seven." He turned to Bobby after ordering. "I drink seven-and-seven on account of the biblical references to the seven plagues, the seven angels, the seven days of creation, and the seven seals of revelation, not to mention how many times Jesus asked us to forgive one another: seventy times seven."

"Well, I drink Bud Light on account of it ain't Coors and they support the gay rags with advertising."

"I'll have to remember to boycott it. Heh, heh. Always preferred Coors myself. Heh, heh, heh."

"That's big of ya, Reverend."

"So you're a homosexual, eh, Bobby?"

"Yes, sir."

"Well, ain't you curious why I'm here?"

"You're one, too, I guess. Frankly, it doesn't surprise me."

"Heh, heh. Not quite, son." And he leaned over to whisper, "I'm undercover. Heh, heh." Then he sat back again. "I'm here to save souls. Do you know how disgusted our Lord would be to look down on this? I've started a new ministry because time is running out. The Rapture is gonna pass right over this place—and not Passover-style either, no sirree. These men here, they're all going straight to hell. And I aim to do something about it."

Just then "Stop! In the Name of Love" blasted out of the speakers. Bobby felt his political ire rising. He was taking a day off from his good behavior and besides, he was in his element. "Reverend, what makes you think that these guys here are interested in what you're selling?"

"I'm not selling anything, son; I'm revealing it. I'm offering it. For free. With a rebate. Money-back guarantee. The lottery itself." His smirk.

Bobby drained the beer and set it down, wondering if the preacher would offer to buy him a second, or whether he should drag the man off his bar stool and to the door. The reverend looked heavy, though. A Herculean task. And didn't Hercules have *seven* labors or something? Maybe he should just start screaming, or blow a whistle ACT-UP style. But no one had whistles anymore.

"The Lord died once for your sins, son. Just once." And he pointed at the Bud bottle.

"What about the second coming?"

"You'll have to wait a spell, son. And better to be sober for it."

Bobby looked at him with disdain. "So how does this work, Reverend? You pick a guy up, take him home, tie him up, and convert him?"

"Whatever it takes, son."

"Let me tell you something, Reverend. Half the guys in here don't believe in your God, and the other half do and they figure Jesus is either queer like them or he just feels the love and supports all this." Bobby scanned the room. "You won't find any souls to save here, Reverend, but you might find a knuckle sandwich. My advice would be to skedaddle."

"Though I walk through…"

"Yeah, yeah.…" Bobby walked away, resolved to keep an eye on the reverend, but also to get what he came for, which just then came stumbling down the stairs in a tattered wife-beater, tattooed like Queequeg, with the kind of scruff that made Bobby's balls tighten and tingle.

The rest of the evening was more or less like most of Bobby's L.A. evenings of years past—a sort of time-suspended circus involving strange leering, smiling faces; a gloopy techno soundtrack; the perusal and exploration of numerous male orifices; the feeling of cold brick against his face, his hands; the hardness of cement on his knees; the burning in his nose, and the rising of frequent belches; the anxieties of, "Did he use a condom? I can't remember," and a chorus of, "Sure for a drink, I will. My name's Bobby," filling his head like a cacophony of advertising jingles. He rode the pinball night in the same way he always had.

It was as he was barreling out the door of the Corner Pocket, his head swimming, sure that the cute boy taking off the discolored, faded BVDs up on the bar was none other than his dear Tony—no doubt full of the gay-for-pay excuse that he needed money for the wedding—when he bumped into Old Croc on the sidewalk. Old Croc was dressed in heaps of rags, and his face shined with sweat. He had friendly, uncannily familiar eyes though, and when they met Bobby's they drilled right through Bobby's frontal lobe like an all-knowing mother's. "I been lookin' for ya," Old Croc smiled.

"What the fuck, leave me alone."

But Old Croc poked at him with his cane as Bobby reeled and leaned against the wall. "The mojo got you, and you'll be dead this time tomorrow if you don't take my mojo medicine."

All the superstitions of his Irish Catholic childhood were roused: black cats, ladders, broken mirrors, and cracks in the sidewalk. Old Croc held out what looked like huckleberries, and Bobby suspected they'd likely kill him on the spot. Not such a bad thing perhaps.

"You better take these or your mojo's gonna finish you off. This time tomorrow. No time to waste. The spirit told me."

Bobby looked at him. He was scared, but his reason told him this man was just a bum looking for a dollar and preying on scared tourists from places like L.A. where voodoo and juju nonsense only appeared in the movies. Bobby leaned down with his hands on his knees, muttering something unsuccessfully to send Old Croc on his way.

"Bobby!" he heard someone call.

Without lifting his hands or torso, he craned his neck and saw a yellow mass moving down the sidewalk. DuMay. "Shit," he muttered, and then he pulled himself up, reeled, and grabbing the huckleberries from Old Croc's open palm, slammed them back like a handful of peanuts.

"Beware of false prophets, son," Old Croc whispered. "Now gimme a little something, and ah promise you, the mojo will leave you be once and for all, and you'll find true love."

Bobby yanked a wad of bills out of his front pocket and proffered them to Old Croc, who quickly snapped the bundle up, turned, and limped off with his carved wooden cane around the corner and down Burgundy Street.

"Get thee behind me, Satan...or in front of me...or whatever," DuMay's voice trailed off as he hurried his girth up St. Louis Street. "Bobby, Bobby," DuMay called out like a lovelorn mother, "God bless you, my son, you are enveloped in the darkness, sick with the tree of knowledge and its foul fruit. But I'm here to deliver you...." And just as DuMay reached him, Bobby's hands went down on his knees again. As the reverend reached out to steady his shoulders, out came an explosive spew of vomit which the reverend was too slow to step aside from, his white loafers showered now in the orange and yellow regurgitated alcohol, Fritos, semen, beer nuts, and huckleberries of Bobby's dismal fall from grace.

Bobby woke up in the megachurch, propped up in a pew, huge metal rafters above him, and DuMay up there at the pulpit, fully wired, his voice echoing and resounding off the metallic walls of what appeared to be an enormous aluminum-sided trailer the size of an airplane hangar.

"I'm down in the trenches with ya, boys. The trench, that's what your kind of boy likes, ain't it? Heh, heh. Face up to it, boys! It's a trench, a foul gutter, an irrigation ditch full of crocs and snakes—all manner of disease, slime, and putridity. The Lord is gonna lift you up. These hands, my hands, will lift ya. And I ain't wearing gloves either. I ain't afraid of your filth. And I'll catch you when you fall, boys. I'll catch ya. I'm a catcher. Heh, heh. BIB, sons, that's what I call my ministry for you all. For the homo-sekshoo-all. BIB. Say it. BIB: Bringing It Back to the heterosexual fold. Bring It Back! Shout it out!" There was a lame muttering of repetition among the sixty or so tortured homosexual congregants. "We're bringing it on and we're bringing it back! And you know what *IT* is, and where *IT* belongs. The Garden, boys. That's what a woman is. A garden. That's what the hoochie is—a garden! Not some toxic Super-fund site like where you're puttin' it! And BIB's the way. Let me fasten that bib 'round your neck, like a bib of righteousness, and when that foul food of the devil drips from your mouth, the bib of the Lord will catch it and keep that pure white Sunday shirt of the second coming clean as mother's precious, holy milk." He pounded the lectern with his index finger. Bobby tried to follow along, but all he could think of were DuMay's fouled white shoes, his sore throat, and the ache in his rectum; his pounding head and burning septum; his parched mouth. "And the Lord, he'll recognize you at the apocalypse. And it's comin'. Mark my words. And there ain't no place at the table for the butt pirate. No, sirree! Now get that bib on! Get it on! Bring it on!"

Something in the reverend's words reached Bobby then, and feeling a surge of energy, he rose, watched the building spin for a few seconds, and once he'd secured his footing, bolted for the door.

Two no-necks stood with folded arms at the entrance, and as Bobby felt more vomit rising, he saw the horrified looks on their faces. They stepped aside and he proceeded to vomit into the cheap, aluminum-sided locked door, which snapped off its hinges as he slammed into it, collapsing like a space shuttle support platform backward to reveal the plane of flooded Chalmette, Louisiana—its upended oak trees and ruined houses, a swath of destruction so immense Bobby could actually see all the way to Interstate 10 in the distance, and made straight for it.

"You can't run from Jesus, boys," he heard the microphone boom. "He's faster than vomit rising. You can't eat without a bib! The world is a trough of sin...You're pigs in it...."

It all faded to an echo as Bobby ran like an escaped convict, ran with all he had, his temples pounding with hangover, his ass aching, tears streaming down his face. My God, maybe he had been born again. But into what he couldn't tell.

He was sobbing by the time he reached the interstate and saw the gas station and the couple arguing. There was only one other customer, a local in a pickup, who soon disappeared into the restroom. He looked back at the couple, the car loaded down with luggage. They were definitely on their way somewhere else. Far from New Orleans—its trailers and mold; its Hacky-Sacking do-gooders and closeted straight boys; its traveler's turds and poorly-laundered BVDs sagging off the gay-for-pay strippers at the Corner Pocket; its fucking gumbo and jambalaya and beignets; its Christian preachers and old men like Croc; its omens and voodoo. It was true. Voodoo. Bobby was pierced full of holes. So what if a good number of the more recent needles were seven inches and made of flesh, or loaded with meth and Jack Daniels? He was poked so full of holes he had to escape or he'd sink like a little gay *Titanic* down into the swamp, never to reemerge.

He was in deep trouble.

Old Croc had been right, and so perhaps was DuMay. Bobby had the sad realization then that when someone was as wrong as him, almost everyone else was right, no matter how harebrained or stupid they were.

The couple kept arguing, the man now back at the trunk, pulling something out and flinging it at the woman. A dildo. She tossed it in a nearby trashcan.

"You happy?!" he shouted.

"Oh, Jeremy," she sighed, and he marched toward her, leaving the trunk open as she burst into tears and he hugged her close. Her head was buried in his chest and his back was to Bobby, who just then got a wickedly convenient idea. *I have to leave now,* a voice said inside his head. Why ask for a ride? Two quick steps and he let himself roll sideways like he'd done in wrestling in high school, and he was in the trunk. But how to close it, and wouldn't they wonder how it got closed? But before he could figure a way, it slammed shut and he heard the man's muffled voice. "It's fucking six hours to Houston; let's get going."

He was elated to be escaping, and escaping seriously, far, far away like so many others had done from New Orleans not a year ago. But six hours in a trunk?

Fortunately, he passed out almost immediately.

He awoke when the car thumped over a dead possum and the woman screamed, "You killed it!"

"He was already dead!" the man shouted back in a slightly high, queer voice.

Bobby had no idea how long he'd been trapped in there, but he wanted out. The trunk was humid, claustrophobic, and smelled like spare tire and Prestone. Within minutes of awaking, Bobby decided that it had been a very bad idea to climb into the trunk, and he resolved to get out as soon as possible.

The rest had done him good, and the hangover had progressed to the stage where a shot or two of whiskey would finish it off once and for all. But for that, he needed to get out. He searched for a latch. Not that he planned to bail out at seventy miles an hour, but just to see if there indeed was one that could be opened from the inside. Perhaps next time they pulled over, he could climb out? Of course, they'd likely just peed and filled the tank when he'd climbed in, so it could be hours. But how long had he slept? He did the math: 15 gallons at 25 mpg = 25 x 15 = ...close to 400 miles. At seventy miles per hour, that was five-plus hours. They might be driving straight through to Houston. He hoped they'd stocked up on sodas and water at the gas station. Shit. A wave of panic jolted through him before it turned to dread. On top of that, he realized that unlike his captors, he now needed to pee. He held it as long as he could. An hour later, the trunk had another pungent odor.

"Good god," Jeremy grimaced, turning his head, "this trunk stinks." Then he saw Bobby curled up in it. "And there's someone in it!"

"What are you talking about, Jeremy?"

"Come here, look!"

"I can explain everything," Bobby muttered. "Please, please, I mean you no harm."

Jeremy look at Jenny; Jenny back at Jeremy.

They helped Bobby out of the trunk, along with their bags, and they took him inside, where they bathed him. "I'll do it, Jeremy!" Jenny commanded him as he began setting out soap and towels, unable to hide the big grin animating his face. "You go watch TV or something."

"Jeez, Jenny, I'm healed, remember?" Jeremy suddenly turned serious.

"Healing, Jeremy," she corrected him, "heeeee-ling." And he stormed past her to watch the *700 Club*.

Bobby was still dazed from hunger, fatigue, and everything else, and he barely stayed conscious through the bath, remembering nothing but Jenny's beaming smile and somewhat disturbing over-vigilance with the sponge, especially in the nether regions. Eventually, she folded him in a towel, doused him with baby powder, and put him to bed, with a kiss on the forehead.

He woke up to their arguing in the kitchen, the sink running, and dishes clanging about.

"Are you gonna be okay here while I'm at work?"

"Yes, I'll be fine," Jeremy insistently and impatiently answered her.

"Can you handle this, Jeremy?"

"Yes, I can handle it!" he retorted.

"Don't get so snappy. I'm just trying to help."

"Well, have a little confidence in me," he relented.

"If I had confidence in you, I wouldn't have done the intervention. You need support, not confidence."

"I need both, Jeanette."

"Just...remember what you learned. This is your Gethsemane. Your cup."

Jeremy thought of PE in junior high when he played goalie in soccer. "My what?"

"This cup shall not pass?"

"What are you saying?"

"I'm saying, this is it, your crucifixion. Do you have what it takes?"

"I'm getting crucified now?"

"Temptation, Jeremy! It's your turn on the cross. God is watching you." And the soft rock station droned on in the background as Bette Midler crooned: "God is watching us, God is watching us, God is watching us...from a distance."

"I'll be fine, Jeanette. You're treating him like he's a murderer or something. I'm strong, have a little faith."

"Him? He has a name! Hello!"

"Whatever."

"See that's the problem, you guys don't even bother remembering names." She audibly sighed. "I don't know. I don't like it. We shouldn't have had him stay."

"What?"

"I mean we don't even know him."

"Christian love? Hello?"

"Christian love? You're not Christ, you're a homosexual who's finding his way back to righteousness, Jeremy. You've got to be conscious of your fragile state. He might be Satan."

"Would you stop?"

"I'm trying to help you!"

"Then leave me be to sink or swim!"

"Sink or swim. Did you look at him? He's a torpedo is what he is. Or a major iceberg. Now I know what they mean by hand-some devil."

"I can handle it," Jeremy half-pleaded. "Now, what's his name?"

"I'm not telling. I feel like I'm leaving a drunk in the house with a case of beer in the fridge. It's insane." She paused. "I should wake him up and take him into town and drop him at the shelter."

"That is so cold."

"You like him, I can tell."

"Oh, please."

"Admit it; he's handsome."

"You clearly think so. How long did that bath run? An hour? Myself, I'm more focused on women and marriage right now. Reverend DuMay healed me, and I'm safe in my spiritual bib thank you very much." Then he added, "And you're gonna be late for work."

"Okay, well, that's the spirit. Keep that bib front and center, Jeremy. I love you." Bobby heard a kiss. "I have faith and confidence in you. Totally. God bless. I'll be home at six."

Bobby waited for the door to close behind Jenny before he emerged, disheveled, in a pair of boxer shorts. Jeremy turned, blushed, and quickly went back to the dishes, barking, "There's coffee and cinnamon buns on the table. Help yourself."

Bobby fell into a chair.

"Excuse me," Jeremy called out over the din of the faucet, "uh...what is your name?"

"Bobby."

"As in Robert?"

"As in Bobby."

Jeremy turned the sink off and began sponging down the counter, his eyes locked on the sponge while he spoke. "Well, Bobby, um, this is a Christian home and we don't come to the table in our underwear. Do you think you could put something on?"

"Sure, but I don't have any clothes, and I don't know what your wife—"

"She's not my wife; she's my sister."

"Oh, uh, your sister. I don't know what she did with my stuff."

"You can wear some of my clothes. Let me get them for you." Their eyes met, both of them blushing now.

"Wow, you're cute," Bobby stated flatly.

"Please. I'm not gay."

Oh, yeah, sure thing, Bobby thought. Maybe he hadn't escaped after all. Bobby suddenly felt trapped again. "You know, I really think I need some clothes and that I just gotta go, like now. I'm kinda confused and uh, a little stressed, and uh...." Bobby couldn't help himself. He started to cry.

"Hey, hey, it's okay." Jeremy took a step toward the table, and then arrested himself. "Don't cry." But Bobby cried. Jeremy carefully sat down in the chair opposite, out of range of any physical contact. Until Bobby reached his hand across the table. Jeremy grabbed it immediately.

"I think I'm having some kind of breakdown," Bobby blubbered.

"It's okay," Jeremy offered, at a loss. Six was a long way off. "Why don't I call nine-one-one."

"I don't need nine-one-one. Just hold my hand."

But Jeremy's pants were full to bursting. "Uh, I can't do that."

"You can't hold my hand?" Bobby looked at him with a face of total heartbreak.

Jeremy blushed, felt a bolt of something rip through his chest, and looked down at the place mat in front of him. "No."

"Please," Bobby pleaded, blubbering, gripping Jeremy's hand more firmly as he began to cry some more. Their hands tangled together hungrily until both chairs went skidding back across the linoleum as they simultaneously lurched forward into a kiss. Bobby dragged Jeremy across the table and they careened onto the floor. Straddling him, Bobby stopped kissing Jeremy long enough to grab his cheeks, look into his eyes, and ask, "Who the fuck are you?"

"I have no idea," Jeremy answered. "Who are you?"

Bobby shrugged. And dove back in.

Pangs of guilt shot through Jeremy as Bobby once again smothered him, and throwing aside everything he'd just learned, he began lustily yanking back the boxer shorts Bobby was wearing. *They are my underwear after all; there can't be any sin in that,* Jeremy rationalized.

They muttered and wept as they communed together and didn't really stop crying completely until they'd betrayed the books of Leviticus and Deuteronomy, as well as Paul's letters to the Corinthians and Romans—and arguably Timothy.

Spent, splayed on the floor together, Bobby spoke first. "I fuckin' need help."

"You need help? If you only knew."

"Oh, I think I know." Bobby leaned up on one elbow. Jeremy looked back quizzically.

"You were lost and wanted to be found—all that shit, right?"

"Something like that."

"Yeah, well, me, too."

"And so, what happened?"

"Well, until ten minutes ago, I was pretty sure it hadn't worked."

"What?"

"Well, you know, like, I'm not a religious guy or nothing. But like, you know the Lord works in strange ways? Or maybe voodoo does."

"Meaning?"

"Meaning I really like you. Like really, really, really."

"I'm not available."

"Uh, well, neither am I actually. I never am. That's what I mean."

"I'm not really following this."

"Well, you know, star-crossed lovers, all that shit?"

"Romeo and Juliet?"

"More like Romeo and Jude, or Jeff, or something."

"Romeo and Jeremy."

"Bobby and Jeremy?"

"I have a dog. He's pretty much my significant other."

"Well, I'm a speed freak."

"I'm a Christian."

"I can't stand Christians."

"I want to be straight."

"I want to move in with you and get clean."

"I want to do what we just did," Jeremy said, sitting up.

"Me, too."

"But I can't."

"But we will."

"No."

"Yes."

And they did.

TOTAL PACKAGE

Michael Bracken

Political correctness hadn't reached my part of Texas back then and the locals still referred to me as a mailman. As a substitute letter carrier, I covered rural routes on a rotating basis, a different one each day when the regular carriers had their days off. Saturdays I ran RR#2 southwest of town, puttering along the shoulder in a right-hand drive Jeep that had seen better days, stopping every so often to fill roadside mailboxes with bills and bulk mail.

I knew more about the people on my routes than they realized. Five-foot-two, two-hundred-and-fifty-pound Ethel May Raditz told everyone she was on a diet but received a package nearly every week from Godiva. Tom Jobe seemed to be preparing for the apocalypse because he subscribed to a dozen survivalist magazines. And Vince DiMarco, at that time the newest stop on the route, had something to hide because he received more than the usual amount of mail in plain brown wrappers.

He wasn't the only one around town with something to hide.

I was so deep in the closet I wasn't sure I would ever find my way out. I'd suspected I was different in high school because I snuck glances at the other guys when we showered, and had no interest at all in the girls—even after Billy Roy Johnson found a way to sneak peeks into their locker room through a hole in the wall of the equipment room—but I'd never told anyone about my proclivity and I had certainly not done anything about it at the time. Not where I lived. Not in rural Texas.

My family didn't have the money to send me off to college, so I worked various jobs around town until I got on with the USPS. Once I had a steady income, I rented a small house three blocks from the station and proceeded to lead a double life. Derek to my family, Rick to most everyone else, I shot pool with my friends at Gully's on Saturday nights, attended the Methodist church Sunday mornings, and spent all of the holidays with my family.

Sexually frustrated because I wasn't interested in the available women my age—most of whom had been through at least one marriage and were either available to every man who bought them a drink or were seeking baby daddies—I sought release during occasional trips away from town. Dallas and Austin became my favorite travel destinations, but after a few years of casual encounters with men who had no interest in sharing phone numbers or last names, I resigned myself to the probability that I would never experience the kind of relationship that my parents—married thirty-five years and showing no signs of wear—enjoyed.

As much as I desired sexual congress with a hard-bodied young man, I wanted something more. I wanted a relationship measured in years and months, not hours and minutes. I wanted the total package. And I despaired of ever finding it.

One Saturday morning, about two months after he moved into the old Denton place, I found myself with a plain brown envelope addressed to Vince DiMarco that had been stamped with a postage due notification. I knew most of the people on my route—I'd gone to school with them or their kin, worshipped in church beside them, or was related to them in some way—so I usually left postage-due mail in their boxes. Charlie Waterson, the carrier who worked Monday through Friday, would find the appropriate amount of money waiting in the mailboxes the next delivery day. But I didn't know Vince. I'd never met him—had never even seen him—and the only things I knew about him, other than what I could discern from casual glances at his mail, was what my second cousin Sally Jo, the real estate agent who'd sold him the old Denton place, had told the family during one of our occasional Sunday afternoon cookouts. He was handsome, single, and worked out of Waco as a claims adjuster for an insurance company.

I glanced at my watch. I was ahead of schedule and nosey, so I eased the Jeep past Vince's roadside mailbox, turned up the short drive, and stopped behind a recent-model Lexus. After killing the engine, I unfolded myself from the Jeep, walked past the Lexus and up the steps to the porch, and leaned on the bell. I heard it clang somewhere deep inside the house. I waited a few minutes and then I leaned on it again.

Just as I was getting ready to leave a pink form telling Vince when he could collect his postage-due envelope from the post office in town, he opened the front door. Wet, ripped, and wearing nothing but a royal blue towel wrapped loosely around his hips, he seemed as surprised by me as I was by him.

His gaze quickly traveled from my white pith helmet down over my blue short-sleeve sport-style knit shirt with the U.S. Mail emblem above the left breast pocket, over my navy blue shorts—worn the regulation three inches above midknee—with the dark blue stripe on the outside seam, over my calf-length blue-gray socks with two navy rings at the top, on down to my polished black work shoes, and then back up to my eyes. Unlike many of my coworkers, I looked good in my regulation uniform. I groomed myself appropriately, took care of my body, bought uniforms that fit, and cared for them as well as I cared for my street clothes.

"I'm sorry," he said, apologizing for his appearance. "You caught me in the Jacuzzi."

I held up the heavy envelope. "This came postage due—"

A black-and-white Border collie shot out the door and grabbed the envelope. My free hand instinctively reached for my pepper spray before I realized the dog wasn't attacking me; it was attacking the plain brown envelope and whatever was inside. For a moment we played tug-of-war with it. Then the envelope tore open and its contents fell to the porch, revealing a familiar magazine, one that I received at my post office box two towns north of the town where I actually lived.

"No, Elroy, no!"

Vince grabbed the dog's collar and wrestled it back into the house as I bent to retrieve the magazine. As he struggled with the dog, Vince's towel dropped to the floor. He wore nothing beneath it and I found myself eye-to-thigh with his muscular legs. His thick phallus and heavy scrotum hung mere inches from my face. If he had experienced any shrinkage from his time in the Jacuzzi, it wasn't evident.

I licked my lips and slowly straightened up with the magazine in my hand, unexpected desire flooding through my entire body.

Vince, still struggling to control the Border collie, made no effort to cover himself. He asked, "How much do I owe?"

I told him.

"I'll get it. Wait here."

He pulled the dog back and closed the door, which pushed

the wet blue towel onto the porch at my feet. I nudged it with the toe of one black shoe, wondering if I should pick it up. I decided instead to step away from the door, and I waited on the edge of the porch near the steps.

When Vince reappeared, he wore chinos and a pale green polo shirt that hugged his thick chest and trim waist. He stepped onto the porch and closed the door behind him to prevent the Border collie from darting out again.

He handed me the appropriate amount of change.

I handed him the magazine.

As he took it from my outstretched hand, our fingers touched. The warmth spreading through me turned into a raging fire. I felt myself stir within my uniform shorts. I said, "I—"

"Yes?" He waited expectantly for me to continue.

My throat was dry, so I swallowed hard and tried again. "I subscribe to the same publication. I—"

Vince looked at me, his dark eyes narrowing as if seeing me for the first time. He cocked his head to one side. "Really?"

I wet my lips. "I rented a post office box a couple of towns over so no one around here would know."

"You haven't told anyone?"

"Not even my family."

"So why tell me?"

I motioned toward the magazine he now held.

"Because of this?"

I nodded. Had I made a mistake? Had I jumped to a mistaken conclusion? "I need to get back on the road," I told him. "I have lots of mail to deliver."

As I turned to go, he stopped me.

"How about dinner?" Vince suggested. "I was going to grill and it'll be no trouble to throw on another steak and couple more ears of corn."

A date? He was asking me on a date? I had planned to drink beer and shoot pool at Gully's with my friends—my clueless friends—that evening, just like I did most Saturday nights. We certainly couldn't go anywhere in town.

"Maybe you can join me in the Jacuzzi after," he continued. "You don't need a suit, and I have a towel big enough for two."

"I—" I hesitated while my mind raced in a dozen different directions at once. I had always sought companionship outside of town. Did I dare take advantage of an opportunity that came to me? Did I dare risk the possibility that someone might see my car parked in front of Vince's later that evening and question why I was spending time with an outsider? I did.

I asked, "What time?"

I returned to Vince's house that evening. I had changed from my uniform into a form-fitting polo shirt, skin-tight Wrangler jeans starched and ironed to put razor-sharp creases down the legs, and well-worn, but not worn-out ropers. Vince wore a light blue, short-sleeve seersucker shirt; tan-colored, pleated-front chino shorts, and slip-on deck shoes without socks. It couldn't have been more obvious that this was a case of country boy meets city boy.

My host led me through the house. I had not been in the place while the Dentons had owned it, but I suspected the interior had never looked so good. The white walls had been recently painted, the hardwood floors had been polished to a shine, and the furniture was sparse but tasteful. Elroy spotted me as soon as we stepped onto the back porch, but the Border collie didn't seem nearly as interested in me as he had been when I was standing on the front porch in my uniform.

"I hope you don't think I've gone overboard," Vince said,

"but you're the first guest I've had since moving in."

He had gone overboard. In the center of the patio sat a glass-topped, wrought iron patio table that had been set for two, with expensive china and real silver. I said, "Maybe a little."

Vince opened a bottle of red wine and poured a glass for each of us. Then he slapped a pair of T-bones and four ears of corn still in their husks on the propane grill and closed the lid. I sipped the wine politely, adjusting my beer-trained palate to the unfamiliar taste.

We made small talk while the steaks cooked, discussing the weather more than anything else, and before I realized how much time had passed, Vince was pulling the steaks and the corn off the grill and preparing our plates.

I sat, he sat, and then we stared at each other.

After a moment of awkward silence, I blurted, "I don't know what to do. I've never done this before."

Vince's eyes widened in surprise. "Never?"

I realized he had misunderstood me so I quickly explained. "I'm not a virgin," I said. "That's not what I meant. I meant I've never done this." I indicated the dinner table with a sweep of one hand. "I've never had a date."

He smiled. "All we have to do is eat."

"I can do that," I said with a smile. "I've been doing that my entire life." Then, between bites, I told him about my trips to Dallas and Austin without providing intimate details.

"And why did you find those trips so unfulfilling?"

I explained about my parents and how I'd always wanted the kind of relationship they had and how I despaired of ever finding it in rural Texas.

"You can search the world over and not find your soul mate," Vince said, "or you can step out your front door and stumble over him."

Is that what had happened?

"What about you?" I asked. "Have you ever—?"

"I was in a relationship for about a year," Vince explained. "I thought he was the one, but I was wrong. Horribly wrong. I had to get as far away from him as I could without changing jobs, and that's why I moved here."

"Is he still in Waco?"

"As far as I know, but there's little chance our paths will cross."

Vince grilled bananas in their skins for dessert, halving them lengthwise and covering the warm fruit with brown sugar and cinnamon after removing them from the grill. We used spoons to scoop the bananas from the skins and before long we were laughing and feeding each other.

After we finished dessert, Vince tossed one of the steak bones to Elroy and then I helped him clear the table and carry the dishes into the kitchen.

I don't know how to explain it—maybe it was the wine, maybe it was the full belly—but I felt comfortable with Vince, so comfortable that we spent the better part of the evening draining a second bottle of wine and telling each other our life stories. He had been out of the closet since his sophomore year of college and I had yet to tell any of my family or friends about my secret life.

"Someday you will," Vince said, "and when you do, no matter what their reaction, it will lift a huge burden from you."

A few minutes before midnight, the second bottle of wine long emptied and the buzz mostly worn off, I excused myself, telling my host that I had church in the morning.

Vince walked me to the front door and opened it. As I hesitated in the open doorway, he told me how much he had enjoyed our evening together. Then he took my face between his hands and covered my lips with his. Surprised but not a bit hesitant, I returned his kiss with equal fervor. As we kissed, my body quivered with desire.

When the kiss ended, Vince stepped back and said, "You'd best leave now before we do something we might regret later."

As I drove away, my jeans so tight at my crotch that I thought the zipper might burst from the pressure, I realized Vince and I had not used the Jacuzzi or his towel big enough for two.

That's how our relationship began, and we spent our next several dates revealing our souls and not our scrotums. In fact, I didn't see Vince naked again until our fifth date, when we ended the evening asleep in each other's arms. By then I knew I had found someone special.

I had found my total package.

THE WANDERER

L. A. Fields

Wade Anderson doesn't remember why he started walking. The decision was made too long past, almost forty-five minutes ago to be exact, and those minutes do not matter anymore. What matters is why he stuck his thumb out and started hitchhiking, but for that he *does* have reasons.

There is the Kerouac in his backpack, the Cash in his ear buds, the sweet smell of gasoline that Wade does not yet detest since he is not old enough to be worrying about gas prices. There is the god-awful monotony of school, the horrors of his small Carolinian town, but mostly, there is the depressing walk between the bus stop and his house, from which he suddenly detoured today. It is nothing but scraggly weeds, tire rubber, and trash (of both the human and refuse varieties), so today he left it behind and headed for the interstate.

Wade is still heading there, but he seriously doubts that he will ever make it. Just let one of the neighbors spot him out here pretending to hitchhike; not only will they pick him up, they will take him straight back home and tell him to quit fuckin' up. *You don't wanna be a fuck-up, doo ya?* He is not so sure lately.

Truthfully, Wade has been going through some changes in his thinking. Now that his first year of high school is almost over, he is thinking he does not want to go back for a second one. And now that the school is abuzz with prom plans (and even the underclassmen can seem to talk of nothing else), Wade is thinking he cannot imagine asking out a girl; he has no goofy butterflies about it or anything, he just does not like girls all that much.

Wade hears a car approaching behind him and he turns to scope it out. He does not recognize it as belonging to anyone who knows him, so that is good, but it doesn't look too promising otherwise. It is a purplish van with an unbelievable glare beaming off the windshield so that Wade cannot make out the driver. He sticks out his thumb anyway, just knowing that the vehicle will not be stopping for him because it is being piloted by some grouchy old wife with eight or nine kids in the back. But to Wade's surprise, the van slows down and pulls over as it passes him, veering close enough to make Wade jump back in self-preservation.

Wade shakes off the shakes and approaches the passenger door. It opens on its own and swings wide, since the van is now inclined on the shoulder. Wade hooks his head inside to see who has stopped for him.

It is another surprise. The bad-tempered mother is not there; it's an older guy (older to Wade, that is, so maybe nineteen or twenty) who looks like California personified to a Southern boy like Wade: he has ocean-blue eyes, sun-blond hair, beach-white teeth, and a palm tree's slender build.

"You almost ran me down," Wade accuses, though his heart is not in it; the muscle seems to have mysteriously stolen away.

"Don't exaggerate. I missed you by a mile," the driver says, punning on the name of the town. Wade has heard the joke before (dear Christ, they all have), but it suddenly seems the height of wit. He smiles wide at the stranger, who after a beat says, "Get in."

Wade does not hesitate, but jumps in and plops his backpack down alongside his butt.

"I'm Darian," the guy says, holding out his hand.

"Wade."

"Where are you going?"

Wade shrugs happily. Hey! He's going somewhere. He already forgot. "Um, wherever you're taking me?"

Darian snorts as he puts the van in drive again. "Good answer."

Wade should be feeling pretty sick about what he is doing, as the sky gets as purple as the van and North Carolina fades into South. He should be worried about how he is going to get back home, what his mother is going to do to him when he shows up a day-and-a-half late, whether or not he will have cops looking for him and what *they're* gonna do to him for running off like this... But he is not worried.

Wade is too busy thinking about sex. The more he finds out about Darian, the more he hopes he is about to be taken advantage of, just like everyone promises will happen if you hitchhike. Darian, it turns out, is not from California, but Florida (*I was close,* Wade thought). Darian is also a musician of sorts, a one-man singer-songwriter guitarist on a "tour," or so Darian defines driving around to random gigs in his stepfather's old van.

That is *so* cool to Wade. He does not know if he knows how to flirt, but he is certainly trying his best, making eyes at Darian and not moving an inch whenever Darian reaches for the radio so that his hand is forced to graze Wade's knee. Darian keeps smiling at Wade, enough to keep him hopeful, but not so much as to give anything away.

By the time they stop driving for the night, Wade is going nuts with wondering. Will he or won't he do something? Is Darian interested in this little country kid? Wade is not about to do a thing in that direction. He will keep himself open, hint broadly if he must, but he will not initiate. Darian seems cool, but you never know how uncool a guy can get until you start hitting on him. He might just hit you back.

Wade need not have worried so much. When they pile into the curiously clean rear of the van to stretch out on the unfolded, bed-sized seat, Darian sets his hand on Wade's thigh, more on the inside than the out, and asks him a telling question.

"How old are you?"

Wade hesitates to say, "Fifteen."

Darian winces but does not remove his hand. "That's pretty young."

"I'll be sixteen in like ten months," Wade adds unhelpfully. Darian laughs. "How old are you?"

"Twenty."

"Oh," Wade says. He does nothing for a few seconds, just kind of waiting around for something to happen. Eventually Darian's hand squeezes him gently and starts to move north. Wade does not stop it. He only watches it closely, too shy to look at Darian's face even though that is the prettiest part of him. The hand stops over his fly.

"First time?" Darian asks.

Wade presses his lips together. "Does it show?"

"Were you trying to hide it? I hope you don't wanna be an actor when you grow up."

Wade looks up to say *Hey* in as outraged a voice as he can

muster with that hand getting so friendly, but Darian interrupts him with a kiss. This is a first, too; the very first of many.

On the last day of school, Wade wakes up in Ohio. He realizes the date because when he turns on the TV in the skuzzy hotel he and Darian are in, it fizzles into the midmorning news and he sees the date down in the corner before he flips past looking for cartoons.

He has been tagging along with Darian for almost two weeks, and if he were a deeper person, he might pause here to take in the concept of time, the futility of measuring such a fluid and magical thing, and to regret that it is running out so quickly. Instead, Wade is just glad that he is not in his English II class right now, counting the minutes and yawning.

He can hear Darian in the bathroom starting a shower. Last night was their first in a hotel. Darian has finally gotten them to his next gig, and he apparently gets a hotel when that happens so he does not stink up the stage with road-funk. That information was offered freely by Darian when they stopped; Wade hardly ever asks a question, and Darian asks none. He does not seem to care where Wade came from, or why he is not there anymore, or even what his last name is.

Wade keeps meaning to tell him everything, but there does not seem to be any rush. For his own part, Wade is surprisingly unmoved by his new transient lifestyle, he is not homesick or worried, and he feels as if he could go on with Darian indefinitely, just drifting along on the road forever.

In fact, that night at the show, Wade suddenly finds himself dying to be a musician. How cool, even at this pathetic open-mic-like gig, how *cool* is it that Darian can play the guitar and sing at the same time? And do both so well? Darian even surprises Wade from up on the not-a-stage platform.

"Okay," Darian tells the ten or so drunk people in the room. "This is a new song, never played it before, and I know that excites you folks, but please try to remain calm." The bartender titters softly, and a tipsy girl up front lets out a long *Owww!*

"Yeah, so. This is for a friend of mine in the room tonight." Darian tips a wink to Wade. "We've been on the road together for a while and, uh… Well, this song is called 'The Wanderer.'"

Darian strums his guitar, tapping his foot to keep the slow, country beat. He whistles forlornly, but clear as glass. He stops for the lyrics:

"When I consider all of the things that I knowed," he sings. "About what's picked up at the side of the road, I think about some folk's garbage and trash, about junkies and killers and counterfeit cash." Darian grins around his words, faking a Southern-ish accent. "But ah never did think about picking up you. That is the one thing that ah never knew."

He is singing the song again when they get back to the hotel, much more softly, and slurred around the edges by alcohol. Wade can taste it on his lips, but that is as close as he will get to a drink. Darian, though perfectly comfortable with his own underage drinking, refused to be a party to Wade's. Totally unfair, to be sure, but arguing was not going to help. Darian's fake ID made him untouchable, and Wade had to content himself with the low level of control he had over Darian's suggestible self.

Now they have fallen on the bed and Darian is pawing sightlessly at Wade's face in the dark. "Hey," he whispers wetly.

"What?" Wade whispers back.

"I love you."

"Oh, really?" Wade is smiling at the gold box of the ceiling in the streetlamp's light.

"Yeah. You smell really good."

"Well, then I love you too. You're a really good singer."

"Thank you," Darian says politely before he falls asleep against Wade's neck in the middle of kissing him. Wade pushes him under the covers and lies next to him, not falling asleep himself, but also not trying to. Wade is just hanging out enjoying the cold blast of the air conditioner, the warmth of Darian's body, and the whole crazy situation. *This is great,* he thinks. *It's just like being on vacation!*

Another week later finds the boys at a rest stop along I-75, Darian turning cartwheels to wake his bones up after driving all day. He groans as his back goes snap, crackle, pop, and then heaves a gargantuan sigh.

"I wish I could take over for a while," says Wade, not really meaning it; Darian looks extremely uncomfortable.

"I'll just bet you do, Useless McGee."

"Anderson," Wade says.

"Hmm?"

"My last name is Anderson."

"M'kay, Useless Anderson. You couldn't have gotten yourself a learner's permit before I found you?"

"I did get one. I just left it at home when I ran away."

Darian stops stretching and comes back to the van, where Wade is sitting on the hood. He puts his hands on Wade's knees and says, "You ran away?"

"Yup," says Wade proudly. "Just took off."

He smiles at Darian, who isn't exactly smiling back.

"Why?"

Wade shrugs. "No idea. Felt like it."

"Um. Okay. Did you leave a note or anything?"

"Didn't have a chance to," Wade says, still oblivious to Darian's concern. "I was walking home from the bus stop and just…" Wade gestures into the distance. "Took a detour."

Darian stares at Wade for a doubt-filled, skeptical second, as if waiting for him to say, "Psych!" When Wade does not, Darian straightens up and away from him.

"What about your parents?"

"It's just my mom. It's not like she misses me."

"What makes you say that?"

"'Cause she's a bitch. She was always snappin' at me to do this and do that and go to church. Fuck that."

Darian crosses his arms and scowls fiercely at Wade. "What?" Wade asks indignantly.

"That's all you've got? She told you to do things you didn't want to do? News flash, asshole, that's what mothers are for."

Wade recoils slightly. "Don't call me an asshole," he pleads.

Darian eases his stance, unknotting his arms and setting his hands on his hips instead. "You could have at least left her a note."

"Well, it's too late now," Wade tells Darian, wishing he had said nothing. Today should have been a silent day.

"You could call her," Darian suggests.

Wade looks around for a pay phone and is relieved when he does not find one. He is about to point this out to Darian when he turns to find a cell phone thrust under his nose. Wade frowns at it, suddenly pissed.

"I'm not calling her. I don't want to and you can't make me."

"I know that," Darian says, not lowering the phone. "But I can leave you here."

Wade flinches like he has just taken a low blow. "You wouldn't do that," he tells Darian, not at all sure if he is right and suddenly scared as well as hurt.

Darian waves the phone at him. "Call your mom and we won't have to find out."

Wade takes the phone slowly, thinking about forgetting the number (Darian would never believe that), thinking about dialing some random number and faking it. But eventually he dials his house and contents himself with hoping that Mom is out.

She's not.

"Hello?" his mother answers. Wade considers hanging up on her. She sounds fine. She is not sniveling into the receiver because her only baby boy is gone; she is not anxiously sitting by the phone waiting for the kidnapper to call. She really *doesn't* care. Wade can totally tell.

But Darian is standing threateningly close, so Wade talks.

"Hi, Mom. It's Wade." And just who the hell else would it be? There is no one else on earth who calls her Mom.

"Wade?" She sounds as if she has misplaced the name. "Wade, is it really you?"

"Yeah."

Wade hears a shaky intake of breath and maybe a whispered *Thank you, God.* "Are you okay?"

"Yeah, I'm fine. I was just calling to…" He looks at Darian.

"To tell her you're fine," Darian whispers.

"To tell you I'm fine."

"Where are you?" she sobs. Her face sounds extremely close to the receiver on her end.

"I'm in, um. I think I'm in Kentucky."

Darian nods as Wade's mother screams, "Kentucky? What are you doing there?"

Wade rolls his eyes. That worry sure lasted a long time; she is already mad at him. He knew she would be. "I'm with a friend," he tells her, really incredibly fed up with this whole thing. "His name is Darian."

Wade's mother starts yelling about something else, but he does not hear it because Darian snaps for the phone. Wade gratefully hands it off and listens to Darian's syncopated half of the conversation.

"Mrs. Anderson? This is Darian. I picked him up. He was hitchhiking. No, I don't. I don't think so. I'm a singer, I... No. No, he's not. No." Darian stops and stares hard at Wade for a long moment. "I think so," he says cryptically.

Darian says "okay" a couple more times and folds his phone up. He slips it into his pocket and walks to the van's side door. "I think we'll stop here for tonight," he says, opening the door, not looking at Wade. He climbs into the van and shuts the door, leaving Wade to watch the sunset, which he hardly enjoys, though it is quite beautiful.

Wade scuffles around, pacing up and down the parking lot, wondering if he is allowed to go inside the van. He feels sick to his stomach, sick at knowing Darian will now look at him differently because he is the kind of boy who would just run out on his own mother, and that apparently is not cool in Darian's book. Maybe he is just really touchy about mothers. His mother probably died or didn't love him or something. That makes so much sense to Wade that he smacks his forehead, goes straight to the van, and climbs inside.

"Hey, Darian?" he whispers.

"Hey, what?"

Wade slides the door shut behind him and feels his way close to Darian in the dark. "Did something happen with *your* mom?"

"No," Darian says incredulously. "Dude, I call my mom every week and tell her where I'm going and what I'm doing and why. Moms like that. Sometimes she'll send me money when I get stuck somewhere with no gas. Or she'll send me extra clothes when I end up north in the winter. Or sometimes she'll send me food, just because."

"Well...then, what the hell?" Wade whines. He does not get what the big deal is, but he wants it to go away now.

Darian shakes his head, sighing. "Maybe you just have to be older to understand?" he asks to no one in particular, since he must surely know that Wade doesn't have the answer. After a lengthy, uncomfortable silence, Darian extends his arm and Wade crawls beneath it.

"I'm sorry," Wade whispers into Darian's hair. He feels, somehow, that he has already been forgiven, but he wants Darian to be sweet on him again.

"Liar. You are not," Darian laughs. Wade stays quiet, smiling but not cocky; he is just happy that everything is all right. "Are you tired?" Darian asks.

"No," Wade says, his smile getting wider with insinuation. Their lips meet effortlessly in the dark.

When Wade wakes in the back of the van a week later, he is unsurprised to see North Carolina outside of the window. There had been a vibe all week, an apologetic but resolute silence on Darian's part that tipped Wade off. He eventually pops into the passenger seat and starts giving Darian directions to his house. Darian says nothing, but he does ruffle Wade's hair gently before concentrating both hands on his turns.

When they get to his house, the door explodes open (it seems they were expected) and from within comes his frantic mother and a flurry of invitations for Darian to stay for dinner, for the night, for as long as he likes. Wade and Darian do not get a moment alone together until the following evening, when Darian is getting ready to leave.

Wade is leaning against the front right fender, watching Darian sift the contents of his van back into proper place.

"Almost ready?" Wade asks.

Darian stops and looks Wade up and down ponderously. "You know you're not coming with me?" He says it as if he is double-checking what he already knows.

"Yeah," Wade says, desultory with the truth. "Where are you going next?"

"Atlanta, then home. For a while." Wade nods. "What're you gonna be up to?"

"Summer school," Wade says, facetiously happy. "I get to retake all my classes if I don't wanna repeat the grade."

Darian shrugs, smiling with only a little sympathy. "Yeah, but whose fault is that?"

"Yeah, yeah," Wade says, being a good sport and smiling back. "Will you come back and visit me some time?"

"'Course I will. Next time I'm around. I can even call you every once in a while."

Through some blip of physics, in the next moment Wade and Darian are in the van, in each other's arms, hugging intensely. They are luckily concealed from the houses on both sides of the street by the van's tinted windows, because neither of them considers the propriety of this display before going at it full tilt. They murmur meaningless shit while they caress each other, but it all matters less than their last kiss—the very first of many more to come.

GUY SYDNEY

David Holly

We met like characters in a Frank Capra film. I was browsing the men's underpants in a downtown department store, indulging in my love for slinky briefs, when I sensed a fellow with a captivating scent standing near. I had just spotted the perfect pair, in tantalizing hues, in the size that fit my curves bewitchingly, and I reached for the package—only to grasp my fellow shopper's soft hand.

"Whoops," I exclaimed, as my fingers met vibrant flesh.

"Oh, sorry," he responded, his fingers still touching mine.

Our eyes locked, and an erotic rush flowed through my body. The sight of him made my thighs burn as if I was leaning against a hot stove.

Nameless yet, he stood, his hand gripping the package that I held, our fingertips sparking a genial intercourse, and I looked into his eyes that mirrored the sea seventy miles distant and his hair that reflected the wheat fields of the Great Plains, and his smooth-shaved skin that personified the purity of snow-capped peaks. He looked more delicious than a great big vanilla milkshake with whipped cream and a cherry on top. *Slurp*.

The enticing stranger seemed as stricken as I, and we released our grip at the same time. The underwear package dropped between us like a shooting star.

"It's yours, take it," he offered.

"How about we share," I quipped.

He laughed musically. "I guess we share a taste in underwear." There was a look of wistful longing in his face. "I'm Guy Sydney." He held out his hand though we were standing close enough to embrace.

I took his hand and held it. "I'm Dick Ryder."

Guy couldn't suppress his smile. Upon hearing my suggestive name, most gay men laughed outright, but Guy had more charm and infinitely more quality. I picked up the dropped package. "I think there are more back here," I said, bending and rummaging through the rack. I found an identical package.

"Just like the other one," Guy said. "It's kismet, Dick. We've known each other two minutes and already we have matching undies."

A chimera of my fancy made my buns wax warm; I covered my confusion by asking, "Want to get some lunch?"

"Sure, Dick." He consulted his watch. "But I have to be back to work in an hour."

"Where do you work?" The image of Guy toiling at some mundane job made me want to cascade into a flood of tears. I could only imagine him as a cup bearer to the gods. Such smooth, soft skin was made for handling delicate philosophical instruments, not for the crudities of earning bread and butter.

"Cabell House. It's a rare book store."

"Rare books?" I breathed in relief; he would fit into a rare

book room or an art museum or as first violin in a symphony
orchestra.

"Yes, collectible first editions. Manuscripts. Antiquarian
imprints. Fine bindings."

"That sounds fascinating," I said. I wanted to lick every
word he uttered.

"Anyway, I promised that I'd be back at one. There's a
gourmet pizza parlor right around the corner. How about we
dine there?"

"That'd be great," I said, lost in a thought wandering through
a dream. If Guy had asked me to eat cheese crackers at a filling
station, it would have been okay. We paid for our underwear
and headed for the pizza parlor.

While we were eating, Guy asked about my job. I blushed.
"It's not a good one and I hate it. I have one master's degree
in humanities and another in library science but when I gradu-
ated, I couldn't find any library hiring. To keep body and soul
together, I took a job as a desk clerk in a hotel. I hate it—I think
I already said that. The pay is terrible and hotel guests treat me
as if they're the slave owners in *Uncle Tom's Cabin*, my fellow
employees are out of *Tobacco Road*, and as far as management
is concerned, everything that goes wrong can be solved with *The
Turn of the Screw*. The current manager is okay, but the horse's
asses at corporate headquarters transfer managers more often
than I buy underwear. Nevertheless, I can't quit because I don't
make enough money to put anything aside, and I have gigantic
student loan payments."

"Oh, my," Guy commented.

"Oh, god," I muttered. What had I done? I'd just dumped the
wretched proof of my membership in the Losers and Slackers
Club on him like a bull raising its tail and dropping chips in the
field. *Plop.* "I'm sorry."

"Don't be sorry." His eyes twinkled.

"I wanted to tell you witty stories about the obscene behavior of the guests and the vile antics of the employees. I didn't mean to say what I said." *Plop.*

Guy looked at his watch. "I must get back to the store."

He wants to ditch me, I thought, but he dumbfounded me by adding, "Want to see Cabell House?"

Maybe I hadn't driven him away. "Right now?"

"If you have nothing better to do."

What could be better? "That's okay?" I asked, amazed that he was still willing to keep me company after I'd come off like Mozart during one of his more obstreperous days. "Your employer won't mind your having company at work?"

"That's not a problem."

Side by side, we returned to the sidewalk. There was a hint of autumn in the air, and a few sprinkles of cool rain fell on us as we strolled. Far from being put off, Guy slipped his hand into mine. Soon we reached a nineteenth-century storefront complete with leaded glass windows.

"Who's your friend, Guy?"

Guy turned to the middle-aged female who was carefully dusting some extremely old books. "Belle, this is Dick. I brought him by to introduce him to the world of antiquarian books. Dick, this is my Aunt Belle."

I briefly took Belle's hand. Guy was eager to show me the bookshop. "Come over here, Dick. Did you ever read Shelley?"

"I had a semester on English romantic poets," I said.

He handed me a small paper-wrapped book. I took it and looked at the title: *Adonais: An Elegy on the Death of John Keats.*

"1821," I gasped, *sniffing clouds of bitter mortality.* "Shelley was alive. How much do you want for it?"

Guy opened the paper cover, and I glanced at the price slip laid in: *$30,000.* I nearly dropped the book. When he picked up a three-volume set, I was afraid to take it. "Are these as expensive as the *Adonais*?"

"Three times as much," Guy replied, knowing eyes blue as the taste of salt. "Take a look."

Setting the books carefully on a table, I first checked out the price. $90,000. The author's name was Robert John Thornton, and the set was titled *New Illustrations of the Sexual System of Carolus von Linnaeus...The Temple of Flora, or Garden of Nature.* The prints were hauntingly beautiful. I fell into each plate like an echo trapped in the shout it mimicked, and I understood why a collector might sell his soul to possess such a treasure.

"Hold on," Guy said. "I want to show you something else." As he stooped to pull out more books, his khaki trousers pulled tight in his cleft, and I saw a magnificent set of curves. *Oh, one touch. Flamboyant buttocks, rich in wheat, great loaves.*

Guy had an encyclopedic knowledge of books, and he must have read everything. After an hour in the store, I was realizing that he was not only gorgeous, but brilliant. I found out that he had a master's degree in literature, and a deep love for all kinds of books. It didn't take long before I wanted to share his world. With Guy, it was more than love at first sight. It was more than just wanting him inside of me, or me inside of him. I wanted to be him.

As Guy gave me a taste of his world of rare books, I kept finding ways of touching him. It wasn't mere lust, though the lust was present, but somehow physical closeness to him was like a potion to me, and I guess I subconsciously thought his magic would rub off.

After a while, customers began to occupy Guy's attention,

two who wanted to buy, and one who hoped to sell. Guy shot me a pleading look as he examined the books.

"I don't want to disturb you," I said, as he halfheartedly studied an immaculate British edition of *Prater Violet*. "I have to work until three tomorrow. Is it all right if I come by after I get off?"

"I'd be devastated if you didn't," Guy said. He wrote his private number on one of the store's business cards and slipped it into a book about book collecting.

When I unlocked my apartment door, a big orange fur ball wrapped its front legs around my leg. I set down my parcels and picked up Maurice. *Buzz, rumble.* He nuzzled me with his big head. Maurice always made my homecomings joyous. After playing with my cat, I stripped to my briefs and threw myself down on my thrift-store couch to study book collecting.

I read about collectors, what they collect and why. I studied the parts of a book, and though I'd been handling books all my life, I'd never known the terminology. I studied how books are printed and bound, and I followed the processes of illustrating.

I baked a chicken breast with carrots and potatoes for my dinner. While my dinner cooked, I cleaned Maurice's litter box. Then I threw away the old newspaper under his food plate and water bowl, put down a clean section of paper, washed his water bowl and refilled it, and fed him on a clean plate. Maurice and I eat off of the same dishes and the exposure hasn't harmed him a bit.

After dinner, I went back to reading about how books were made and marketed down through the centuries until I came to twentieth-century first editions. Fascinated, I read on until the phone rang.

"Hi," he said. His voice was melodious, even fruity, but the strawberry tones enhanced his charm.

"Hello, Guy," I answered. "I'm reading about books."

"Did I get you hooked?"

"In more ways than one," I ventured.

I heard a sharp inhalation followed by a pause. In spite of the gift book, I hadn't fully realized that he was as smitten with me as I was with him.

"I really liked the bookstore," I said.

"Thanks."

"Does it belong to your aunt?

"No, Dick, the shop is mine. I work and live in it. Actually, just overhead. I live in the apartments above the bookstore."

I was embarrassed, but I understood why he had been cautious. Obviously, he had money, just as it was obvious that I had none. I might have been a gold digger, but he was throwing caution through the windowpane. "You talked like you just worked there. You didn't tell me you owned the place."

"Yes, my father was a bookman, and he left me this shop. Aunt Belle works for me, just as she worked for her brother." Aunt Belle must have earned more in a month than I managed to rake in over the year.

"Thank you for trusting me," I said, warmed by the flattery implied in his truth.

As I talked, I was lounging on the couch in a T-shirt and bikini briefs with black and green horizontal stripes. My briefs stretched and grew hotter as Guy's voice entered my ears and sallied from cell to cell until it suffused my whole flesh. I considered telling him about my condition, but decided not to offer my sexual favors too quickly.

"I was reading about points of issue when you called."

"Would you like me to come over and explain the points more fully," Guy asked.

Yes. Yes. Yes. I surveyed my humble surroundings, and my face flushed. If he saw my apartment, and found out that I was easy to boot…and Maurice picked that moment to jump on my stomach and butt my chin with his head.

"Oh, Guy, I have to get out of bed at five." I paused before adding hopefully. "You'll see me tomorrow afternoon."

Guy sighed. *Ahhh.* "You promise that you'll come by when you get off?"

"Sure, I already promised."

"Have you ever been to a book auction?" Guy asked. "I have to bid on some books at five tomorrow."

"If you're inviting me, sure. That sounds interesting. I've never been to an auction."

We talked for another hour. After we hung up, I was afraid that I'd have trouble sleeping, but I drifted off immediately and had pleasant dreams until the clanging alarm nearly threw me out of bed.

Still attired in the previous day's underwear, I plugged in my waffle iron and mixed waffle batter, using more egg yolk than the recipe required, and a touch of vanilla extract. My first waffle cooked while I spooned Fancy Feast onto Maurice's plate, warmed it in the microwave, and added dried cat food.

While Maurice was eating, I dropped hunks of butter onto my waffle and covered it with dark buckwheat honey. Twenty minutes later, I was dressed in desk clerk uniform: dismal gray slacks, an undistinguished blue blazer with the hotel logo, and the hideous striped tie. I shuddered at my mirror image and hurried to the light-rail stop.

I worked alone behind the desk for the first several hours. I checked out large groups of rushed guests, dealt with a

ridiculous number of phone calls, and solved countless prob-
lems. Naturally, unreasonable humanity expected every task to
be accomplished immediately.

At eleven-thirty, swing-shift employee Belinda arrived, big-
haired and made up like the Bride of Dracula, not to mention
half-hungover and walking bowlegged. Belinda had been due
at eleven, but she was late as usual and looked like the scratch
of fingernails on a chalkboard. Before I'd wished her a good
morning, the desk phone rang.

Belinda loved the phone better than life itself. Soon she was
flirting with some caller as if she'd known him for years. While
she was talking, I checked out guests from the last fifteen rooms,
and coordinated the rooms already cleaned with the house-
keeping department.

Finishing my shift, I dumped my hotel uniform in the
employee bathroom and changed into the clothes I had brought:
a pinkish-hued dress shirt and olive slacks that highlighted my
assets. An arriving waiter was changing at the same time.

"Dick, did you hear?" he said, glancing cockeyed at my
burnt sienna–colored bikini underwear. "Ms. Brooks is getting
transferred." Ms. Brooks was the general manager, and my
heart sank at the rumor. She had always treated me well. We
had gone through a succession of managers during the two years
I had worked at the hotel; the good, the bad, the stupid, and the
criminally insane. Ms. Brooks had been better than most. If the
course ran true to form, the next manager would be an imbecile
working on becoming a bastard.

The auction house was a long building with huge doors swinging
open from both ends. The bidders sat in a gallery of seats while
the auctioneer stood at a podium, crying items while young
men and women raced to and fro with heavy objects. Guy and I

walked a long row of tables that extended the full length of the auction house. Lots 250 through 325 were books, and though the auction had been progressing for several hours, the books were not due for crying until five.

Attendants on the opposite side of the table opened each box as Guy approached. Most he gave a cursory glance and passed on. Lot 289 caught my interest—somebody had marked *Tarzan* on the side. I nudged Guy so he asked to examine the contents.

The attendant placed the eight novels before us. The books looked old, but they could have been printed yesterday. The paper was creamy white and the dust wrappers bore only minor tears. I picked up *At the Earth's Core* and beheld Edgar Rice Burroughs's signature. *The Outlaw of Torn* was not signed, but *The Chessmen of Mars* had been a presentation copy to a friend, signed merely Ed. In spite of the label, there wasn't a Tarzan in the box.

"They're fascinating, aren't they?" Guy said.

"They're beautiful."

"You can find paperback copies," Guy suggested.

"I don't want to read them. The writing is crap. But they're works of art as they are."

Guy hugged me. "You've got the idea. Collectors don't buy these books to read."

"They buy them to drool over," I finished. "Or as an investment."

Guy said. "You're the first date I've brought to an auction. I never before met anybody who understood."

That was my first glimpse into his soul. I saw loneliness. Here was a brilliant man, cultured, literate, appreciative of letters, living a sad, lonely life because he'd never met anyone to share his interests. I imagined that he had had lovers in the past, some perhaps who pretended a fascination with books. But each lover would prove more interested in parties, bars, or bathhouses.

I too had been viewing Guy with shallow eyes—or rose-colored glasses—for I had been enthralled by his air of knowing the world, his suave gayness, and his good looks. Still, I assured myself that I was different from past lovers. I too had a taste for letters.

We passed along the table, examining books but none closely until we reached Lot 311, a box labeled nonfiction. Guy inspected each book before handing it to me. They were beautiful; even the ones that did not interest me, interested me, especially one titled *A Monograph of the Pheasants*. While I examined the *Pheasants* and *The Birds of Washington,* Guy devoted most of his attention to Harry Clay Palmer's *Athletic Sports in America, England and Australia*. By the time we had finished examining Lot 311, the auctioneer was crying the first boxes of books.

To my surprise, Guy bid three hundred on Lot 262. He had scarcely glanced at that box.

A fat fellow with a loathsome beard raised his bid, and Guy dropped out when the bids reached five hundred. Fat beard ended up the winner, but it cost him nearly $750. Guy didn't raise his paddle again until Lot 289, the Edgar Rice Burroughs novels, came up. I wanted him to win, but my heart leaped into my throat when the bidding started at $4,200 with a woman in scarlet making the first bid. Guy bid $5,000 and a third bidder promptly raised the bid by $500. Guy did the same, so the scarlet sister jumped the bid to $7,000.

"Too much, too much," Guy moaned. My heart sank, but a thrill shot through me when Guy abruptly bid $8,000. The woman in scarlet had suffered enough at his hands. She bid $10,000, and I could see that Guy had shot his final bolt. He had bid that last thousand because I liked their dust jackets. I felt a rush of heat. *Sizzle*.

Guy didn't bid again until the crying of Lot 311. The auctioneer started the bidding at $3,500. Guy scanned the crowd for his competition, but they were curious in their absence. I wondered if everyone else in the room knew something that Guy didn't.

After a deadly silence, Guy raised his paddle and bid $2,500. Then he had the room's attention. Several bidders whom I guessed were also book dealers started whispering furiously with each other. Meanwhile the auctioneer was conferring with several people.

"I'm sorry, Mr. Sydney," the auctioneer said deferentially. "The minimum bid is three thousand."

"I'm sure that's what the seller wants," Guy called, "but I'm willing to write a check for twenty-five right now. Unless someone wants to bid against me?" He made the last part a question, which resulted in a flurry of buzzing but nobody else raised a paddle. *Whisper, whisper.* An assistant gabbled into a telephone, and I guessed that the seller was hanging on the other end. Abruptly, the assistant nodded.

"The seller has lowered the minimum bid to twenty-five. We have a bid. Do I hear three thousand? Twenty-eight hundred? Going once. Twenty-six? Going twice." *Bang.* "Lot three-eleven sold to Guy Sydney of Cabell House for twenty-five hundred."

We stopped at a desk where Guy wrote a check. A rather cute young man, probably with a doctorate in art, lugged the box to Guy's van. We thanked him and headed back to Cabell House. On the way, I reached into the box and pulled out several of the books. Replacing *A History of Playing Cards and a Bibliography of Cards and Gaming* and *The Clock Book; Being a Description of Foreign and American Clocks*, I puzzled over *Athletic Sports.*

"Open it to page four forty-six."

I read an excerpt from a speech by Mark Twain.

"I've never seen this speech."

"No one has," Guy gloated. "This is a lost work. I don't find it mentioned in any of the Twain bibliographies."

"What was Lot two sixty-two?" I asked.

"James Branch Cabell first editions," Guy said.

"Your bookstore is named after him?"

"Hardly anybody reads him today, but he was considered one of the America's greatest writers. 'The optimist proclaims that we live in the best of all possible worlds; and the pessimist fears this is true.'"

Sunday afternoon we dropped in on an estate sale, which turned out to be much ado about nothing. The blustery promoter huck-stering the estate had promised Guy a case stuffed with first editions but the books turned out to be worthless book club copies.

"That was disappointing," I commented as we drove away without adding a single book to the inventory of Cabell House.

Guy laughed. "Rare books live up to their name."

"Meaning they're rare?"

"How true," Guy confirmed. "Dick, if memory serves, you're off work tomorrow."

It was about time he mentioned my schedule. I'd been dropping not-so-subtle hints all afternoon. *Love me, love me, love me.*

"Would you spend the night with me?" he asked, working up his nerve. Perhaps my attempt not to appear too easy had been overdone.

"Yes," I agreed. "But I have to run home and feed my cat."

"Don't run. We can drive."

My mind reeled. "Guy, my place is awful. I live with gloomy lighting and thrift-store furniture."

"I buy books from thrift stores, Dick," Guy said. "Do you think me such a snob?"

Suddenly the words gushed from my mouth. I told him how I feared that he'd think me a gold digger. He bought $10,000 books whereas I was an $8.79 per hour desk clerk. Guy stopped my fears with a kiss. *Ahhh.*

When we entered the apartment, Maurice sniffed Guy's ankles. Guy stroked Maurice behind his ears where he likes it so much, and my undignified cat flopped onto his back with all four legs in the air. I wanted to follow suit.

Guy picked him up. "A neutered male. Declawed. Maurice looks like a good bookstore cat." Maurice agreed with a purr that I could hear above the sound of the wheezing refrigerator.

While I fed Maurice, Guy studied the books on my shelves. At least I wasn't ashamed of my taste. My books may have been cheap paperbacks, but they were literature, the better mysteries, and several works of the highest quality science fiction. Guy barely glanced at my threadbare rug or my twenty-dollar couch.

I promised Maurice that I would stop by in the morning. The cat gave me an accusing look, as though he knew I was abandoning him for a night of pleasure in Guy's bed. Feeling vaguely guilty, I walked arm in arm with Guy to the van.

We ate stuffed flounder at a seafood restaurant before returning to the bookstore. We entered through the front door, and Guy locked it behind us. Then he led me through the back to a flight of stairs leading to paradise. *Ahh, yes, Guy, ohhh.*

So the weeks passed. I spent my mornings at the hotel desk, and my late afternoons in the bookshop or scouting with Guy. The search took us everywhere. I endured the slings and arrows of Belinda's catastrophes until three, and then I fled to nirvana.

Nearly two months expired while we awaited our new boss. I saw the new manager briefly on the day he arrived. He looked like a young Groucho Marx. My bad feeling increased when I learned that he would be living in one of the hotel rooms. He surveyed the lobby and the dining room, radiating an aura of smug intolerance. As I checked him in, he assured me that he was going to get the place whipped into shape. *Smack, smack.* I was not reassured when he selected Belinda to show him to his room.

That evening Guy and I dined at a popular restaurant. "Can you stay with me tonight?" Guy asked.

"Can you wait until tomorrow night, Guy? The new manager is taking over tomorrow, and I'm nervous."

"Why?" he demanded. "You're the most efficient employee that dump has."

I could scarcely disagree. "The night auditor tells dirty jokes to the guests, the maintenance guy is drunk all day, and the breakfast cook is an anarchist who fantasizes about poisoning the guests. But Belinda is the biggest problem. Maybe the new manager will make Belinda pull her weight."

The next morning I checked out ninety-five guests who questioned their bills in languages I couldn't speak. Naturally, Belinda arrived a full hour late. As I was trying to explain the telephone charges to an Arabic-speaking gentleman, the desk phone rang. Belinda grabbed it up and told me that I was wanted in the back office.

The new manager was drumming his fingers on his desk as if I had taken a side trip to Baja. His nameplate read *Ron Repp*. I was relieved that he did not offer to shake hands.

"Dick Ryder," Ron Repp said, his lip curling as he scanned a file folder. "I see that you've received two reprimands." His voice was a backed-up septic tank.

"They were bogus," I retorted. "One was for overbooking the hotel, and I don't even take reservations. The sales manager overbooked us and then made certain that someone else got the blame."

"Fixing blame is the province of the Human Resources department," he rebuked me. I already knew that fixing blame was the only thing that HR was good for.

"I find a notation that you are a homosexual," he said, his vocal cords tightening upon the word so he squeaked like a rat eating Limburger.

"My sexual orientation is listed in my personnel file?" I protested. "Is that legal?"

Ron Repp's face purpled. "I don't appreciate your attitude. Our company has a nondiscrimination policy, but that doesn't give you the right to flaunt an offensive lifestyle in front of our guests."

My heart was thundering. "Flaunt? Offensive lifestyle?" I gasped weakly. I felt like H. P. Lovecraft receiving Cthulhu's thickest tentacle.

"You need retraining. I'm going to have Ms. Victor work with you, and she will report to me regarding your progress or lack thereof."

I couldn't believe my ears. "Belinda Victor commits ninety percent of the major screwups, then I catch the guest's rage. Twice she's managed to book two guests into the same room."

"There isn't a blemish in Ms. Victor's file," he said. "I must tell you, Dick, that your future with this company is insecure."

Three o'clock finally arrived, but not before Belinda had told some guest the wrong time for the shuttle to the Expo center. Three minutes before I was due to clock out, the inconvenienced guest read me the riot act. So loud was he that Ron Repp came to the lobby to watch the guest dress me down. After the guest had departed in a taxi at the hotel's expense, Repp jotted a couple of notes on a pad, and I assumed that he was planning my letter of dismissal.

I was shaking by the time I reached Cabell House. However, the sight of Guy examining a hoary tome with a magnifying glass restored my humor. Guy was attired in white slacks—a little less slack than the current fashion (I liked that)—and a pink short-sleeved shirt. He was beautiful, and I drank in the vision of his sensuous shape while he was yet unaware of my presence. Then Belle nudged him and pointed at me. Guy looked up from his book and his face broke into a radiant smile, brighter than sunlight on fields of poppies, and as heart stopping as a rainbow.

Before I knew it, Guy had swept across the room, hugged me tighter than a rambunctious python, and planted his lips on mine. His kiss was long and lingering, and my tongue met his. The front of my olive pants bulged obscenely.

When we came up for air, Belle cleared her throat. "Boys, should I pull the blinds and lock the door?"

Guy laughed musically and dragged me behind a counter to conceal our erections from his aunt—too late. "Hardly that, Belle." Then he winked at me. "Besides Dick and I have the whole night before us."

I worked with Guy until the store closed at seven, and he continued my education by showing me examples of pirated editions and false firsts, primarily cheap editions from China designed to imitate the publisher's copy, or book club copies printed from the same plates at the first edition, but upon cheaper paper.

"How about dinner?" Guy asked as he pulled the blinds and locked the front door after the last customer.

"Yes, but I have to feed Maurice."

I had not neglected my cat during the weeks of my courtship, but I was feeling guilty. Maurice had been sleeping more the past week, and I was afraid that he was lonely. I rolled a golf ball down the hallway until he tired of chasing it. Then Guy brushed him while I warmed Fancy Feast in the microwave. Maurice did not care for food directly from the refrigerator, and nine seconds was sufficient to release the savory odors.

While Maurice ate, I picked up my phone and heard the message tone beeping. My heart rose into my throat as I heard the callous voice of Tamara from Human Resources ordering me to report to her office at nine the next morning. My day off.

"Dick, what's the matter?" Guy asked.

"I better take a rain check, Guy," I said, tears leaking from my eyes. "I might not be good company tonight."

Guy embraced me and then sat me down on the sofa. I filled him in on my encounter with the evil Ron Repp.

"They're going to fire me," I cried. "Because I'm gay. Even though they have an antidiscrimination policy, they're going to blame me for other people's screwups."

"If they fire you, they're doing you a favor," Guy said. "Come spend the night with me as you planned. Bring Maurice along with his food and litter box. And ignore the phone call. Don't show up at the HR office tomorrow."

It didn't take much urging, and I spent the night in Guy's bed with Guy cuddled up to my back and Maurice warming my chest. I didn't go to Human Resources, but spent that day with Guy at an estate sale while Belle managed the shop. When we returned with a van loaded with highly collectible books, I saw Maurice sleeping in the front window as if he'd been working in a bookshop all his life.

Over fillets and au gratin potatoes that night, Guy offered me a job at three times my hotel wages. Then we spent half the night making love in all the dreamy, wonderful ways that two fellows can perform with each other, while Maurice sat on the end of the bed and watched approvingly. *Meow.* Afterward, Guy asked me if I would give up my apartment and move in with him. *Yes, I told him, yes, I will, yes.*

The morning after my two days off, I dressed in my hotel uniform and reported for my shift as if nothing had happened. Ron Repp, accompanied by Tamara, the soul-slaying HR demon, ripped into me as I entered the lobby.

"I called you in two days ago," Tamara shrieked.

"First I heard about it."

The pair practically dragged me to the HR office where Tamara threw termination of employment forms in front of me. Included was a promise that I wouldn't sue them, which they expected me to sign in return for my final paycheck. I removed my hotel blazer and necktie and laid them neatly on Tamara's desk. "Please sign the form that proves I returned my uniform."

"After you bring us the pants," Tamara said snidely. Her jaw dropped when I stood up, removed my trousers, and laid them on her desk. "Everything else is mine," I said pulling up my shirt-tail to expose my green and white striped bikini-clad butt to Ron Repp. *My underwear felt like the scent of a field of cucumbers.* Repp's face turned so dark and the veins stood out so alarmingly in his forehead that I thought he'd pop his aorta.

I walked through the lobby in my underwear, past the wide-eyed Belinda behind the desk and several slack-jawed guests, carrying my termination papers including the unsigned agreement not to sue and minus my final paycheck, proof that Ron Repp and Tamara had violated three state laws. I maintained my dignity down to the curb where Guy sat waiting in the bookshop van.

"You were right," he chortled. "They did literally strip the pants off of you."

I pulled on the slacks that I had left in the van, while Guy examined the photograph he had shot of me exiting through the lobby door. "Our lawyer is going to love this picture," Guy said.

Our lawyer was aggressive in pursuing gay discrimination cases, and the hotel settled for $100,000. The lawyer got half, but I didn't care. I wasn't suing for the money so much as I wanted the hotel to treat future employees—particularly the gay ones—better than they had treated me. I paid off my student loans and ploughed the remainder into inventory for Cabell House, and I eventually became Guy's partner in business as I had already become his partner in life, love, and sex.

For the past five years, Guy and I have run our rare book store together, living above and working below. Day by day, we have lived with the dreamy companionship of rare books and each other, and night by night, we have whiled away the time in love—watched closely by Maurice. We have an idyllic partnership to which, save for the separation we all must make, neither of us can see an end.

THE FOOD OF LOVE

Jay Mandal

Three rather tipsy-looking terra-cotta pots stood wedged in a homemade wooden frame on the worn, sand-colored cobbles. A young bougainvillea grew to one side. Behind the pots was the whitewashed wall of the villa, its blue shutters flung open, the sash window pushed up. The interior looked cool and inviting.

Sam was hot. He wasn't used to this sort of weather. Of course, it was better than the depressingly constant rain he'd left behind in England, but he longed for something to quench his thirst and maybe a dip in the sea.

If he'd kept going to the gym, then he might not be suffering like this, but he'd let his membership lapse along with his New Year's resolutions. He sought comfort in food: cakes and biscuits, suet puddings and crumbles. He ate because there was no one special; and there was no one special because he ate.

He'd come on holiday by himself. Everyone else seemed to be paired up. He didn't want to impose, so he went sightseeing on his own. On this particular day, he'd decided to see some murals that were mentioned in his guidebook, but he hadn't reckoned with the heat. He mopped his brow. As he rounded the next corner, he caught sight of his objective: the church. It stood at the top of the hill, bathed in sunlight. He sighed, and trudged on.

It was cool and quiet inside the church. Sam admired the murals, and spent a few minutes looking around. Then he realized that he wasn't alone. Sam hesitated. Not wanting to disturb a genuine worshipper, he decided to leave. He was making his way out as unobtrusively as possible when he tripped over something. A man glanced up.

"Sorry," they both said at the same time.

"My rucksack—I shouldn't have left it there." The man got to his feet. "Are you all right?"

"I just banged my knee. It doesn't hurt." Sam tried a few steps.

"You're limping."

By unspoken agreement, they headed toward the door and made their way down the hill toward the car park.

"This is mine," the stranger said, unlocking a Renault rental car and putting his rucksack in the boot. "Which one's yours?"

"I walked."

"Well, you can't walk now."

"I'll be all right," he said stoically.

"Let me give you a lift. It's the least I can do."

Sam was tempted. He supposed you don't often meet mad axe murderers in a church. "Okay. Thanks," he said.

"Andrew Smith." The man held out his hand.

"Sam Taylor." Andrew's grip was firm, his smile friendly. Sam blushed. Flustered, he forgot he was abroad and opened the driver's door.

"I'm sorry if I've I spoilt your day," Andrew said, once he was in the driver's seat and he'd established where Sam was staying.

"It was getting too hot for sightseeing. I kept thinking of that song. You know, 'Mad Dogs and Englishmen'..."

Andrew reversed out of the parking space, and they headed back to Son Bou. The journey passed all too quickly.

"Here we are, then," said Andrew, as he pulled up outside Sam's hotel.

"Would you like to come in for a drink?" When there was no immediate reply, Sam rushed on. "I expect you're busy." He opened the passenger door.

"No."

Sam was confused. "No, you aren't coming in or no, you aren't busy?"

"A drink would be great." Andrew locked the car, and followed Sam into the hotel.

The bar was deserted. Sam had an idea. "Let's have a drink by the pool." He led the way outside. "*Voilà*! What can I get you?"

They sat under a parasol and sipped their cold beers. The swimming pool beckoned invitingly. Sam sighed contentedly. "I've spent the last hour or so longing for this," he said, raising his glass. "Oh, and to go for a swim."

"The water would probably help your leg. Hydrotherapy."

Sam's eyes lit up, then clouded again. "I can't abandon you."

"I've got my trunks in the car," said Andrew.

"Mine are in my room," Sam replied.

Sam dived into the still pool. The water was heavenly. He swam a couple of lengths then turned over and floated on his back, his eyes closed.

"How do you float like that?" said a voice. Startled, Sam

sank, and came up spluttering. Andrew was treading water a yard away from him.

"Fat's lighter than muscle."

"You're not fat. You're just right."

Sam wasn't used to compliments. Was Andrew chatting him up?

"People are obsessed with their weight," Andrew continued. "Fashion has a lot to answer for. Who wants someone who's just skin and bone?"

Sam nodded. How could he admit that he was one of those people obsessed with their weight? It was all right for Andrew: he probably never put on an ounce whatever he ate.

They spent a pleasant afternoon between the bar and the pool. Sam asked Andrew if he had to be somewhere. Andrew replied that he had nowhere important to be. Besides, he was enjoying himself. Sam had a warm feeling in his stomach then wondered if he'd drunk too much.

It grew late. Sam was hungry, but he didn't know how to broach the subject. It was Andrew who eventually suggested finding somewhere to eat.

They went to change.

Sam dithered between casual and smart. Then he began panicking in case Andrew lost patience. He emerged from the lift still putting on his watch. "Where to?" he said breathlessly.

"There's no rush. We've got all night."

All night?

Nearby was a restaurant with a menu that they both agreed upon. Once inside, however, Sam was torn between chicken in a rich sauce with sautéed potatoes, and tuna with salad. The tuna sounded the healthier option, but the thought of the creamy mushroom sauce made his mouth water.

The waiter was looking at him.

"Chicken, please." No willpower.

Andrew ordered the tuna. "I hear the local fish is excellent."

"Oh, it is! Very good for you."

It wasn't long before the waiter brought their meals.

After a while, Sam noticed that Andrew was staring at him. "Have I got sauce on my chin?"

"No. I like to see a man enjoying his food."

"I enjoy it too much," Sam said, patting his stomach. "'Oh, that this too, too solid flesh...'"

"You've no cause to worry." Andrew toyed with his food, then put down his knife and fork and declared himself full.

"You've hardly eaten anything. Didn't you like it?"

"It was fine," Andrew said halfheartedly.

"This is delicious," said Sam. "Try some."

Andrew speared a piece of chicken. "Sublime," he pronounced.

"There's far too much for me."

Andrew needed no further encouragement.

Afterward, they ordered apple strudel with cream. And two coffees.

Andrew sighed contentedly, as he put his serviette on the table.

"I don't suppose you'd like a nightcap?" Sam asked.

Andrew smiled. "I'm sure you'd look very fetching in a nightcap." He glanced around. "Is it me, or is it sleepy in here?"

"On second thought, perhaps we'd better get you home."

"Your place or mine?"

"Mine's nearer."

"Such impatience!" Andrew gave Sam a lascivious grin—thereby removing any doubts Sam had about his sexuality—before sliding off his chair and under the table.

* * *

With the help of the waiter, Sam got Andrew back to the hotel room. There, they put him carefully down on the bed. The waiter left, Sam's thanks ringing in his ears and a five euro note clutched in his hand.

Only then did Sam realize he was exhausted. He undressed down to his boxer shorts, and climbed into bed beside Andrew.

A giant stick of celery was pursuing Sam across Brighton beach when he was woken by an arm flung across his chest. The events of the preceding night flooded back. What would have happened if Andrew had remained sober? What, more pressingly, was going to happen now? He did not have to wait long, as the body beside him gave a convulsive twitch, groaned, and muttered what sounded like: "Never again."

Everything went quiet for a few minutes. Then the hand on Sam's chest began to move. Sam tried to ignore the tickling sensation.

The next moment Andrew was sitting bolt upright. "Shit!" he said. He gazed wildly at Sam. "Did I...? Did we...?" There followed a string of apologies. "I don't usually behave like this. I don't know what came over me."

"We were both a bit drunk. Well, maybe more than a bit. Nothing happened."

"Thank god for that!" Andrew obviously realized that could be misinterpreted. "Although I'm sure it would have been fantastic."

"How are you feeling?"

"I could do with a shower to wake me up."

"Be my guest." Sam led Andrew to the bathroom and showed him how the shower worked.

"I don't suppose you'd like to share it with me?"

Sam pretended to mull it over. "Well, they're always saying we shouldn't waste water."

Afterward, as they lay in bed, Andrew reflected on the rapidity with which he'd passed out. "It must have been those new tablets the doctor prescribed. I shouldn't have had any alcohol while I was taking them, but I was nervous."

"Why were you nervous?"

"Having a meal with you."

"You think I'm scary?"

"Of course not. You're cute." Andrew hesitated. "It wasn't just you. It was the food, too. It was all so tempting. But, if I'm not careful, I put on weight. I weighed seventeen stone when I was twenty-one. I lied, you see. All those things I said...they apply to me. My name is Andrew and I'm a yo-yo dieter."

Silence.

"I'd better go," he continued, getting out of bed. "I've lied to you and got drunk." He collected his discarded clothes.

"And what we did in the shower? Was that a pretense, too?"

"That was real. I do care."

"And I care about you, too," Sam declared firmly. "I'd been afraid you were going to tell me you had a partner. We can help each other. We have so much in common, although I'm fatter."

"You're not fat, Sam. If you were thinner, there wouldn't be anything to put my arms around."

Sam was moved, but there was something he had to explain. "You're not the only one who lied," he said slowly. "I let you think I had a limp when in fact there was only a stone in my shoe."

"Why did you lie?"

"We'd only just met and I thought you'd drive off into the

sunset and I'd never see you again."

"I didn't realize you were so devious. I can see I'm going to have to keep my eye on you. Don't worry about the limp thing. I know a great cure. Follow me back to the shower!"

LONELY BOY

Doug Harrison

M y pace quickened as I strode from my parents' car. I
glanced back once. Dad waved from the driver's seat,
a nonverbal gesture of support nurtured by his desire for me
to begin the life experience he never had. He lowered his arm
and flapped his hand, figuratively pushing me forward, as he
had literally done many times before to urge me onto the field,
any sports field. Mom also waved, sorta, a weak gesture, her
hand wavering between encouragement, blowing a final kiss, or
wiping a tear.

I heard the familiar sound of the engine sputtering before
turning over. It was no longer a family car—I was on my own.
Carless and clueless. I suppressed a chuckle. My motor mind still
coughed up phrases like a nondescript character in a Gilbert and
Sullivan operetta, but at least I was near Boston, home of the
Lamplighters. Not that I would have time or means to wander
off campus— I'd come here to study physics and math, and that
was that.

I snickered. Julie was sure in for a surprise. No more dating, even though she was majoring in voice somewhere in the bowels of Boston. So she won the Best Voice in New England Contest—got a full-time scholarship. Big deal. I didn't win any Best Science Student Contest, but I had dug up a scholarship too. I wondered how she was doing during her first week in town. Probably lonely like me.

I winced at the memory of the unending stream of compliments I had shoveled into her voracious ego, and the memory of my inevitable reward—going home with lover's balls, my jockeys glued to my upper thighs with precum. I was wedded to my right hand. Well, to both hands, since I had such a big dick.

Who had the big ego now?

I rubbed my crotch, and then quickly withdrew my hand, hoping no one had noticed. My mind flashed back to the dark corner of the magazine section of my hometown's sole smoke shop, where every month I had crouched over the latest copy of *Physique Pictorial*, pressing my hard-on against the chipped wooden display case, peeking at hunks clad in posing straps. The few nude models with hard-ons didn't outrank me in endowment, but their physiques sure did. God, how I had yearned to look like them. Did that make me queer? I sure wished prissy Julie had given me the chance to find out.

I bit my lower lip. Fledgling students and their parents flowed around me as if I were an implacable boulder in a turbulent stream. No one smiled or said hello. And, of course, I didn't make any effort to engage them.

Then a guy about my height pushed his way toward me: brown hair, like mine, but close-cropped, a tailored crew cut. His freshly pressed sport shirt didn't conceal his gymnast's physique. He held out his hand.

"Hi, I'm Mark. You a new student?"

I stared at one of my suitcases, then the other. "Yeah," I mumbled. "I'm Brad Chapman."

Mark unrolled a single-sheet scroll of paper, glanced at it, and shoved it into his hip pocket. "I'm one of the brothers from Alpha Pi Omega, over there." I followed the smooth arc of his hand across a grassy field and past a cluster of tennis courts to a row of brick buildings. "We volunteered, well, it was our turn this year, to welcome the frosh and get you settled in. The guys, that is. The sorority sisters help the women." He leered. "And point them toward the frat houses."

I managed a weak smile.

"C'mon, let's get started." He turned, faced the building I had been reconnoitering, and swept his hand in a grandiose semicircle.

God, was this guy a drama student?

"You must know this is Samuels Hall," he said.

I nodded and scanned the *U*-shaped, ivy-covered, weathered-brick building. Its three floors rang with the creak of stubborn windows forced upward, doors slamming, and a few shouts of joy. A long banner, made of wrinkled white sheets held together by large safety pins, displayed a scrawled message: WELCOME, CLASS OF '61.

"A couple brothers from the house cobbled that together," Mark volunteered.

At least they tried, I thought. *Four years, four long years of...of what?* My mood was ironically underscored by Elvis's big hit, "Heartbreak Hotel," blasting from a corner window. I wondered if I dared tune in my favorite program, *Live from the Met*, every Saturday afternoon. I lifted my suitcases.

"I'll take those for you."

Before I could protest, he yanked them from my hands. I wasn't sure if Mark suppressed a laugh at my bargain-basement luggage, but I sure did notice the bulge of his well-tanned biceps. I followed him up two flights of stairs, past communal bathrooms, to a three-room suite, my home for the year, like it or not. We entered.

A rail-thin man several inches shorter than me introduced himself. "I'm Jim."

"And I'm Sam," grunted the second.

They both held out their hands and we shook.

"We took the room over there," Jim announced.

A third freshman meandered out of the second bedroom. "I took the lower bunk in the other room. I'm Winston." He walked back into the bedroom and resumed his unpacking. I took in the undersized living room—two small desks with matching chairs that probably creaked, and an overstuffed easy chair that needed a stitch job. I went into my room: one desk.

"I took the desk," Winston announced without looking up as he arranged pens, pencils, and a few mementos from home on the small surface. His open designer suitcases occupied most of the lower bunk. I stared at the upper bunk: no ladder. Good thing I'd hiked miles of rocky terrain and learned to hoist myself over obstacles. Mark swung my suitcases onto what was to be my nightly precarious perch, a nest with one occupant.

"Well, here you are," Mark said, and again offered his hand. "If you need anything, give me a jingle." He handed me a scrap of paper. "That's the house number." He smacked me between my shoulder blades, but his slap lingered and his hand slid a few inches down my back. He strode toward the bedroom door, quickly scanned the living room, and smiled at me, a smile that lingered like his slap as his periscope gaze traveled from my face to my feet and back to my eyes.

I blushed. He left.

I scrutinized the bedroom. The bunk beds were shoved into

an alcove. Two bureaus and Winston's desk filled the opposing
wall. His monogrammed towels were neatly folded over the two
towel racks screwed into the back of the door.

Shit! No goddamn privacy. I could retreat to the library to
study, but where would I jerk off? In the shower? In the bushes
at night? I'd managed at home with Mom and Dad downstairs.
But I didn't have three roommates there, and I wasn't forced
to share an upper and lower jammed into a tiny bedroom to
boot. Could I manage a silent quickie under the covers? Would
Winston notice? Would he smell my cum? Would he even care?

The four of us finished unpacking and found our way to
the cafeteria. I filled my tray with my first nondescript college
dinner; Jim, Sam and I sat together chatting about where we
were from, this and that, but Winston spurned us for a group of
guys wearing prep-school blazers.

After dinner I paid my respects to Jumbo, a huge stuffed
elephant—P. T. Barnum's gift to the school—that was part of
college lore. Jumbo was ensconced appropriately in the foyer
of the biology building and was conspicuously anatomically
correct. I placed a quarter in his curled trunk, as my dorm mates
had told me we freshmen were supposed to do, and returned to
my room to collapse onto my high-rise bed.

Winston, already in pristine underwear, had taken off his
black horn-rimmed glasses and was in the act of inserting
earplugs. He switched off the light as I entered. I flicked it back
on and flicked him the bird at the same time, threw one set of
his towels onto his desk, placed my towels on the rack above
his, brushed my teeth, and hauled myself into bed. I tossed and
turned while Winston snored, and I vowed to find a drugstore
the next day to purchase my first set of earplugs.

No more waking up with a warm cat nestled in the crook of
my legs. My coffin-sized enclosure sat over the lair of a selfish,

entitled Grinch. The pleasant vibes emanating from a purring cat had been supplanted by sizzling stress, much like a high-tension wire crackling in the night.

The next morning found me seated in a large lecture hall in the physics building. At eight fifty-five, a tall man with a medium build, thin glasses and a crowlike plume of thick dark hair entered. He wore a rumpled, brown, threadbare tweed jacket, despite the early fall heat. He ambled toward the center of the long lecturer's platform, stared at his captive audience, and stepped into the wastepaper basket. None of us moved a muscle as he leaned over, grabbed the container, and yanked his shoe free. He scrutinized the room as if nothing had happened.

"I'm Professor Knapp, chairman of the physics department. I'm pleased to see so many aspiring physicists in the freshman class. More than we've ever had. I'll spare you the cliché of, 'Look to your right, and look to your left,' but the truth of the matter is, only a third of you will graduate with this major. But welcome anyway." He pointed to a pile of papers on the table. "Take one of these. It's a list of your respective advisors. Good luck." He left the room.

With the help of a map, I found my advisor's office and we worked out my courses for the first semester, the usual for a physics major, except I talked my way into a sophomore philosophy course. I again consulted the map, and headed to the gym to register, where an assemblage of tables on the basketball court, sprouting raised signs like delegates at a political convention, announced each department. I likened the maelstrom of milling students to the interior of a confused beehive. Nonetheless, I obtained signatures for all my class choices and collected the appropriate booklists, then headed for the bookstore.

My physics text was the first in a three-volume set, but I

grabbed all three hefty tomes so I could browse ahead to assuage my curiosity about upcoming topics, especially during the summer. My philosophy text was the two-volume boxed set of the complete dialogues of Plato. Would Plato even hint at Greek homosexuality, and if he did, would the instructor skedaddle around it? Math, German and English lit texts quickly followed, until all that remained to pick up was my gym uniform.

I approached the only likely counter to face a young female student, not much older than me. *Shit!*

She grinned. "You want a gym uniform, huh?"

I stammered a soft, "Yes."

She looked at my chest. "You take a medium, huh?"

An even softer, "Yep."

She reached under the glass counter—could she see my crotch through the display case?— and said, "You'll need one of these." She pushed a box containing a size-large jock toward me. I blushed and went to the register.

An older woman rang up my purchases. I used my new check-book for the first time.

"All your books won't fit into one bag," she said. "Not even two."

"I'll just carry them," I said. "But can you put these in a bag?" I bunched my gym jersey, shorts, and jockstrap into a clump behind the books.

"Yeah, sure." She smirked. Salesmen selling bras had to control their reactions better than that.

And with that, I started across the campus, my books stacked precariously in my arms, held from the bottom at waist level, the paper bag with my gym equipment tucked between the top book and my chin. I was reminded of the giants in *Das Rheingold* sealing off the last vestige of Freia with a final golden brick.

I was staggering across the quad between bookstore and dorm when I spotted Mark walking toward me. He waved and broke into a trot.

"Here, let's put those down," he ordered as he maneuvered books and me to the grass. The tower of books toppled. I sat cross-legged amid the wreckage. Mark sat opposite me, leaned back on his elbows, and laughed. He wore black running shorts that accentuated his crotch as he spread powerful legs. His flexed biceps flowed into muscular shoulders that gripped the tops of firm pecs. His nipples and washboard stomach were outlined through a tight, sweat-soaked red singlet. A grungy white face-cloth dangled from his shorts; he yanked it out and threw it to me. I wiped sweat from my forehead and tossed it back. We caught our breaths and stared at each other.

"Quite a load," he observed.

"Yeah," I answered.

He looked into my brown paper bag and grinned. "I'd like to see you in that."

"They're just gym shorts."

"I mean the jock, man."

I blushed for the second time that day.

"You have great calves," he said. "Do lots of running? Let's back up, what sports are you into?"

"I'm no athlete. But I did develop into a good swimmer at summer camp." I took a deep breath. "So, I tried out for the swimming team freshman year. Within a week I had the worst case of athlete's feet the family doctor had ever seen. Had to soak my size elevens in purple glop twice a day for ten days. So that ended that. But, I figured, running can't be too different from swimming, just opposite body parts moving in sync. Hell, anyone can run around in circles—well, ovals, to be precise. Got to be pretty good. But the guys made fun of me, like, skinny and all that. Hell, I always thought runners were supposed to be thin. Well, it was the *sissy* part that really got to me."

Mark grimaced. I continued.

"I'd go to the track after practice to run solitary laps and I'd gaze at the hills as the setting sun cast long shadows. It was very peaceful."

"You're poetic," Mark interjected.

"Thanks. We lived in a valley, a typical New England factory town built up around a river, and I'd walk a mile home from school up steep hills. And often, weather permitting, I'd hike in the woods."

"You're quite something," Mark said.

"Well, along with being a nerd, I do like nature. Especially since trees and brooks don't poke fun at me. The gift of nature is that she returns, indeed amplifies, whatever you give her."

Mark leaned back, his hands under his head, bunching his biceps, and stared at the sky. Then he sat up.

"Like to go on a hike tomorrow?"

My mouth dropped. "Er, yes. Where? No, I mean yes, but wherever you want to go."

"Ever hear of the White Mountains?"

"Of course. I've read a lot about Mount Washington, the cog railway, the two-hundred-mile-an-hour winds at the top, fierce weather that can change in an instant. And Franconia Notch and Crawford Notch. And Lucy Crawford and her loneliness."

I paused after the last word. Silence hung between us like a sheet of glass, a transparent barrier.

Finally Mark spoke. "We'll start out easy—Mount Chocorua. Bring a jacket and be at the house at six a.m. I have a car and I'll take care of the food."

I blanched at the early hour. "Can I bring anything?"

"Just yourself." Mark stood, grabbed my hand, and hoisted me to my feet. "Back to the dorm with you." He grabbed most of my books, I took the remainder and my brown bag, and we moseyed to my room.

Winston, attired in spotless plaid Bermuda shorts and a tailored polo shirt, looked up when we entered. Mark and I deposited my books on the unclaimed desk in the living room; he said, "See you tomorrow," and left.

"*I* didn't have anyone to carry my books home," Winston snorted. He raised an eyebrow. "Where are you two going tomorrow?"

"Hiking."

"You mean walking in the woods?"

"What else, numb-nuts?"

Winston cut short a comeback, looked at my stack of books, and sneered, "Christ, you've got a lot of books. What're you majoring in? Have you even decided?"

"Of course. I knew what I wanted to study when I was in high school. Physics."

"Physics! What the hell is that good for?"

"Oh, it's led to a few things here and there, like electricity and airplanes."

"Well, I've got lots of thick books too. I'm premed. My dad's a doctor."

"And what's your specialty gonna be? Have you even thought about that?"

"Of course! Whatever makes the most bucks."

No Albert Schweitzer complex there. Better living through med school. I dashed into the bathroom to piss.

"Christ," I yelled. "There's a goddamn fish in the shower. A big one!" I dashed back into the room.

"Yeah," said Winston, hands on hips. "We each got our

specimen today for biology class. It's on ice. We're going to dissect it this semester."

"Ice or no ice, it smells," I yelled.

"You'll get used to it."

I went nose to nose with Winston. "I thought you biology creeps started with worms."

"We did that in high school. Go shower downstairs."

Jim came out of his room. "You gonna name it?"

"Goddamn!" Winston shouted and stormed out, probably to have dinner with his preppy friends. I felt like pitching his frozen fish after him.

That night I climbed into bed. Winston was already snoring. I thought about Mark. I sure would have liked to see him naked. Probably looked like the full-size reproduction of the discus thrower statue in high school. Of course, Mr. Thrower wore a fig leaf, but so what. He looked like a *Physique Pictorial* model. I retrieved an unused wad of Kleenex from under my pillow, spit on my right palm, and coaxed my boner to a hardness I seldom achieved.

"What're you doing up there?"

"What d'ya think?"

"What?" Winston must have pried out one earplug.

"I said, 'What d'ya think?'"

"Stop shaking the bed, you woke me. Go get off in the bathroom."

"And come all over your goddamn fish?"

"Fuck off!"

"That's what I'm doing, asshole!"

"Well, don't dribble on me."

"Get over it—go back to sleep. I'm almost done, anyway. To paraphrase Gilbert and Sullivan's Nanki-Poo, 'You've interrupted a private apostrophe.'"

"What the hell does an apostrophe have to do with jerking off?"

"You'd never get it, jerkoff."

The next morning my alarm went off at five-thirty, much to Winston's annoyance. I showered in our bathroom, notwithstanding the stinky fish, which I shoved to one side. Winston would be pissed when he discovered his soapy, thawing fish.

Mark met me in dawn's semidarkness at his frat house door. He turned on the porch light, aghast.

"You can't hike in your gym shorts!"

"They're all I have. Besides, they're brand new."

He waved me in. "C'mon upstairs. I'll set you straight." I followed him to his room. It was surprisingly large and had a small bathroom.

"How'd you rate your own bathroom?"

"I'm the house treasurer, and a junior," he stated matter-of-factly. "Now, get out of those shorts." I turned to go into the bathroom. "Hold on," he ordered, "I've seen it all before." So I stepped out of my shorts in front of him.

He took a hard look. "So, I finally get to see you in your new jock," he said. I blushed. "Nice. Now let me see the bottoms of your sneakers." I put my hand on the back of a leather recliner and raised my legs one at a time. He examined my soles, coming close—deliberately?—to brushing his shoulder against my crotch. "Okay, I guess they'll do. If the terrain was really rough, you'd have to get a good pair of hiking boots."

From his bureau, he retrieved a pair of long, dark brown walking shorts with deep side pockets. The material was durable, almost like corduroy.

"You can slide halfway down the mountain in these, and not tan your ass." He winked. I stepped into the shorts and ever so slowly buttoned my fly.

"Let's go!" Mark thrust his backpack into my hands and we went into the kitchen. He grabbed a small cooler and led me to his car, a red '55 Ford coupe. He opened the trunk and plunked the cooler near the front. I noticed several coils of rope, white, black, and red, and what I assumed was climbing equipment, like carabiners.

"We're not going to repel?" I squeaked.

"Not to worry. No cliff walls. Not this time, anyway."

We drove to New Hampshire, chatting along the way about our interests, hometowns, boyhood friends, and old girlfriends. His current girlfriend was also a junior. He didn't say much about her, but probed me at length about Julie until I vented my frustrations about not getting any. He nodded; he'd been there, apparently.

Finally Mount Chocorua came into view. "I'm going to take you up a fairly easy trail, but one that tourists usually don't bother with," he said as we pulled into the parking lot. Mark slung his backpack over his shoulder, and we started up the Champney Falls Trail.

The air was nippy in the early morning autumn air, but soon heated up. After a couple of hours, we stopped by the falls, rested, and drank from the water bottles clipped to our belts. Mark took his shirt off and splashed cold water over his torso. I stared at his body. I couldn't help myself.

"Well, what're you waiting for?" he asked. I slid out of my shirt. "Nice," Mark said, and splattered me with cold water. We played around like two kids for a spell, then resumed our hike, finally passing the tree line to an upward sloping field of open rock. We clambered up, Mark in the lead, occasionally turning to see how I was doing, and offering a helping hand when needed, which wasn't often. We reached the top, rewarded by a breathtaking view of forested hills, rocky ravines, and craggy summits.

We were alone. Mark eased his backpack off.

It was almost noon, and the sun was directly overhead. Mark was well tanned, but he applied lotion to my shoulders, back and chest. I closed my eyes and sunk into his caresses, and we both sighed when he capped the bottle. A warm breeze embraced our half-naked bodies while we watched cumulus clouds drift among distant mountaintops, occasionally jostling for position around the peaks. Mark put his arm around my waist and pulled me close.

"There's a lot to be said for a breathtaking view when you earn it."

I murmured a husky *yes* while encircling his waist with my arm. His hand slid into my rear pocket just as we heard voices. Mark shook his head, moved away from me, and pulled a large red beach towel from his backpack. We sat cross-legged, smiling at each other while reveling in the view. He handed me a piece of cheese, I don't remember what kind, and then two wineglasses and a small bottle of wine appeared.

"Liebfraumilch," he intoned as he opened the bottle and poured. "Virgin's milk," he added through a sly smirk. "White and fruity."

A party of four had arrived, noticed us, and settled onto a far boulder. They acted like a pair of newlyweds with their kissing and fondling. I was jealous of their freedom. We finished our meal, relaxed for a few moments, cleaned up, and headed back down the trail.

The descending trek was more rapid than the ascending hike; we were about half an hour from the car when the trail forked. Mark counted a number of measured paces and stopped. He pushed his way a few feet into the dense foliage and signaled me to follow with a flick of his head. We were still shirtless. I was sure his arms and chest were getting scratched, but I was close behind him and didn't get nicked, his knapsack notwithstanding, when the bushes snapped back into place. We came to a grassy clearing, about ten feet in diameter, and Mark halted. I pictured a doe and her faun nesting for the night in this secluded spot, surrounded by an almost impenetrable thicket. Mark lowered the knapsack and again spread the large beach towel, this time with the knapsack under one end to serve as a pillow. He rested his hands on my shoulders.

"You know I'm attracted to you."

"Yes. I can sense it. I...I feel the same way about you."

"I'm going to give you your first real kiss."

I studied my shoes, hoping Mark wouldn't notice my tears.

"Don't cry," he said. "Not now. Sometime, but not now."

I nodded.

He lifted my chin with his forefinger, took me in his arms, and we kissed. Our lips formed a grotto in which two tongues lingered, searched, and caressed.

We took a breather, literally, and I began to kneel, unsure how to proceed, but willing to explore the possibilities. Mark put his strong hands on my shoulders.

"Lie down," he said, his voice a gentle command. I complied. He stood at my feet and stepped out of his shorts. I gasped.

"You've been waiting for this, haven't you?" he asked.

I couldn't speak. There he stood, clad in jock and boots, the quintessential centerfold from *Physique Pictorial*, except that the bulge in his jock was pulsing.

"It's okay, it's okay, relax," he said. He knelt and slid my shorts and jock over my sneakers. My cock *thwapped* as it bounced off my abdomen. Mark stripped off his jock and his dick, mimicking mine, sprung out and up. He lowered himself onto me and ran his fingers through my hair. I shuddered. He wiped a final tear from the corner of my eye.

"This has never happened to me," I managed to say.

"You've dreamt about it, haven't you?"

I nodded, and giggled.

"What's wrong?"

"Nothing. I'm just happy. Even though I've been taught that this is wrong. Very wrong."

"Maybe it is."

"I've tried to be with girls, but...but..."

Mark put his finger across my lips. He took me into his arms and held me. Tight. I shivered. Then he ran his index finger the length of my torso, tracing the fine line of sprouting hair from the center of my chest to my navel. "You're beautiful," he murmured.

"I'm so skinny," I countered.

"You're okay just the way you are. Besides, you're filling out. Sign up for weight lifting in gym class if you must. But I'm drawn to your innocence, your inner beauty, your purity of soul, your sincerity."

I gulped.

"You may lose your innocence, but hold on to the rest."

He pressed his lips to mine, and I melted. I again yielded my mouth to his tongue, a symbol, hopefully of a beginning, of me offering my body, my essence, my spirit.

He gently moved my arms from my sides and placed them in a crosslike position. Then he locked his hands onto my wrists. His sinuous thighs forced my legs apart and snared them in a spread-eagle position. I couldn't move. Mark ran his tongue over each of my nipples. I moaned. Then he nibbled and bit. I yelped as my dick twitched. Pleasure and pain. A new sensation. Oh, yeah, I had played with my nipples now and then. But this was different, very different. A sweaty man, a gorgeous hunk, had captured me. He was on top of me, our dicks pressed together by our firm abs.

I looked past Mark's face. It was no longer high noon, and the sun's rays filtered obliquely through pine needles, down to variegated leaves, in the first blush of fall.

I climbed the pyramid, naked and sweaty, prodded to its flat top. I was spread-eagled on a sacrificial stone, four priests in multi-colored loincloths and flaming plumed helmets stretching my limbs to their limit. The high priest approached. The obsidian blade gleamed in the sunlight. I screamed. Why? I submitted. I arched my back slightly and offered my heart to the knife. My pulsing, bleeding heart was held up to cheering crowds far below.

I knelt in church, my hands clasped in prayer. I stared at the painting of Jesus, rays of light emanating from his bleeding heart.

I couldn't give my heart to Mark—he had already taken it, and knew it. He lowered his head to my cock, and licked the tip. My imagination had never conjured such sensations. He swallowed my dick, all of it. I arched my back and pumped into his face. My body trembled. Mark raised his head, releasing me. His eyes followed the arcs of our cum, combining in a pool of ejaculate on my stomach, glistening like dewdrops in the sun.

Mark held me as our breathing slackened, then crawled next to me and put one arm under my shoulder, holding me with one hand. He ran the index finger of his other hand through the silky slickness of my belly and licked his finger clean, his tongue pausing on his lips to savor the taste. He scooped up more of our cum and offered me his finger, a silent communion.

We cleaned off, using our jocks. He stood and pulled me to my feet, offering me his jock as he stepped into mine. His wet pouch clung to my soft dick and I cupped my fist around it.

"Our own secret," he whispered through a smile.

I grinned. "Like a wedding ring."

The bushes rustled and I jumped.

Mark laughed. "Not to worry. Just a squirrel looking for nuts, not a skunk or a bear."

"Or a person," I added.

"We're safe here." He paused and lifted his finger to his chin like a mischievous kid plotting some evil. "Next time I'll bring my rope. The soft rope."

My spent dick sprung to life. Mark moved behind me, reached around my shoulders, and rubbed my chest. His hard dick in the damp jock probed my buttcrack. I moaned and clasped his hands. "It's time to start back to campus," he said.

"It's silly, but I wish we could hide in our secluded nest forever."

"You're not silly."

"Forbidden love is usually challenged, often doomed, and sometimes fatal," I whispered.

Mark spun me around. "Where did you get *that*?" His hard dick bobbed within the tented jock like a reproaching finger. "Sounds like you should be majoring in philosophy or ethics."

"*Tristan und Isolde*," I answered.

He looked perplexed.

"An old legend. My favorite opera." I paused, regrouped, and continued. "A more modern version is *Lady Chatterley's Lover*."

"Yeah, class differences."

"Yep. Class differences. Sexual preferences weren't even mentioned then. At least not openly."

"Still aren't, Kinsey notwithstanding," Mark concluded. "C'mon, let's go." He shook grass, dirt, and pine needles from our red towel. He flicked his head for the second time that day.

I latched on to the opposing corners of the makeshift blanket and we reverently folded it into a red cube, resting it in Mark's upturned palms. It was warm from the heat of our bodies. He looked into my eyes with an unblinking stare. I placed my hands on top of our portable nest and we leaned into a final kiss.

He lowered the blanket into his rumpled rucksack, brushed the creased surfaces of the bag with measured motions, and slid it over his sweaty shoulders. Unlike Tristan and Isolde, our lovers' afterglow didn't lead to round two of heightened passion. Not that day. We trudged back to the car, each lost in his own thoughts.

MAKE A WISH

Rob Rosen

It was my birthday, the big two-five; dinner at a new restaurant, something low-key. Just a few close friends and ample quantities of booze to help usher me out of my twinkhood. The place was packed solid, sardine-can tight, with loud hipsters, louder music, and a strange oceanic decor. We were seated dead center, at a small table, our elbows bump, bump, bumping. Not our usual surroundings, not by a long shot.

"Why exactly did you guys pick *this* place?" I asked my friends, not as graciously as I probably should have, all things considered.

They smiled, shrugged, and replied in unison, "Hot waiters."

"Ah," I ah-ed, fingertip to nose, a nod of my head. "Got it." And I did.

I looked around, however, and none were in sight. Go figure. And then, seemingly out of nowhere, "Good evening, gentlemen. Can I take your drink orders?"

I glanced over my shoulder, my gaze taking in long, tapered fingers before it moved up a hairy forearm, to a starched white shirt, broad shoulders, and finally, *gulp*, to eyes the color of the sky just before sunset—a pristine blue, startling in their intensity; radiant.

"Gin and tonic," I squeaked out. "Light on the tonic."

He grinned, revealing teeth as white as fresh mountain snow, straight as proverbial arrows. I gulped again. Time, as they say, stood still, the din surrounding us receding before switching to mute. The only presence I now felt was his. *Kaboom*, went my heart as he wrote our orders down. "Coming right up," he announced, turning around and walking away, his perfect ass swaying to my heartbeat. *Kaboom*: my heart again, threatening to explode.

I looked at my friends, my mouth agape. "Told you so," they all said, with knowing smiles.

"Fuck," I managed. "You guys saw him too? I wasn't hallucinating from lack of food?"

They shook their heads, one of them replying, "No, but I'd stop eating altogether if that was the case."

I laughed, the clamor around us turning back up to a normal pitch, the universe righting itself upon his departure. But not for long. Oh, hell no. He returned lickity-split, drinks in hand, smile in full force. My mouth went dry as the Sahara. Good thing he set my cocktail down first; I drained it in two gulps, my thirst unquenched.

"Ready to order, gentlemen?" he asked, his voice tumbling over me like a crashing wave, pulling me in, dragging me under.

Shell-shocked, I hadn't even looked at the menu. "Steak," I blurted out. "Rare."

He laughed, the wave washing over me again. "Um, this is a sushi restaurant, sir."

"Oh," I oh-ed, suddenly understanding the Japanese-style furnishings. "Then, um, tuna. Raw."

My friends ordered their meals while I tried my best not to stare at his firm jaw, lined on either side with a soft brown fuzz, and then back to his eyes, sparkling like sapphires beneath the dim lighting. I truly tried. And failed. Miserably. "And another round," I added, just before he turned away.

He put his hand on my shoulder, flesh on fabric, the heat searing through. "In a jiff, sir."

And then, to my profound dismay, he was gone. My heart skipped a beat as I again turned to face my friends. "Did he just say *jizz*?"

"Jiff, Jeff," I was corrected. "Back in a jiff. Geez, get your mind out of the fucking gutter."

Gutter nothing. My mind was in a wedding chapel, with white doves flying out of a three-tiered cake, the photographer telling us to say cheese. "Oh, um, yeah. Jiff." A wave of red rushed up my neck, flushing my cheeks as it sped across my face, a brush fire that swept its way down to my pulsing cock, now ramrod straight against my thigh. It wasn't that I believed in love at first sight, necessarily, but lust was a whole other kettle of fish—pardon the expression.

The rest of the night went by mostly in a blur, crystal-clear only upon our waiter's sadly too-infrequent returns to the table. Not that I ate much; my heart was galloping past my stomach by that point. I excused myself toward the end of our meal, pleading a need for the restroom, but I went out the back exit, desperately in search of fresh air to help me unscramble my much-addled brain.

I shut the door and turned around. All was pitch black beyond the reach of the dim overhead lighting. "Hello?" I whispered, certain I heard breathing beyond the wee cone of brightness.

"Hello." A man's features emerged from the darkness. "Just taking a break. Did you need something?" Our waiter's head tilted, his smile reappearing.

Oh, fuck. His laser-intense eyes bored through me. "Oh, um, no. I was, um, taking a break, too." I laughed, nervously, looked away, briefly. "Birthdays can be so, um, *exhausting*." I leaned against the door for much-needed support.

His smile widened, the area around us suddenly a hundred watts brighter. "Well then, happy birthday," he said, his voice rising as he lifted his hands in hearty congratulations. He stepped closer, his minty-fresh breath mingling with my gin-infused breath. "Did you get everything you wanted?"

The question hung in the air, tinged with something instantly recognizable: desire. I locked eyes with him. "Great food, good friends, strong drinks. What else could a boy want?"

His grin mirrored my own as he closed the gap between us, his lips meeting mine, soft like a cloud, his tongue darting, snaking and coiling its way inside my mouth, and we swapped warm, wonderful spit. "How about a birthday kiss for the boy who has everything, then?" he whispered after he withdrew his tongue, the palm of his hand caressing my cheek.

"Oh, yeah. I'll have another," I whispered back, all smiles, nearly breathless. His arms pulled me in and I fairly melted as something hard poked me in the groin. I reached in to cop a feel. "Chopsticks," I groaned. Just chopsticks.

He pulled away, his smile ever-present. "Which reminds me, I have to get back inside." He ran his fingers through my hair, tracing his way down my face, my neck. "Sorry."

My own smile faded. "Yeah, no problem. Thanks for the um…"

"Birthday present? My pleasure." He winked and reached for the door, saying over his shoulder, "Name's Glenn, by the way."

"Jeff," I hollered back as the door clicked closed behind him, echoing in the darkness that abruptly enveloped me. "And, man, are *you* getting a good tip."

I waited a few seconds as my breathing returned to normal and my hard dick settled back into place, and followed him inside. I sat and finished my meal, the burn of his lips lingering on mine. And there he was, at my side, a bowl of coconut ice cream in his upturned hand, a candle burning atop. He set the bowl down. "Happy birthday," he said, leaning into me, blowing warm swirls inside my ear, sending a shiver down my spine. "Make a wish."

I shut my eyes good and tight, made that wish, then opened my eyes and puffed out the flickering flame. My friends applauded, toasted me with the remnants of their drinks and wished me well. And our waiter did so again, his hand on my shoulder, adding a subtle squeeze that sent an emotional burst through my body. I looked up, my smile as big and bright as his. Whatever I was feeling, he was feeling too. No mistaking it.

Soon afterward, dinner was over, the plates cleared, the bill paid. Waiter Glenn disappeared into the kitchen as my friends ushered me into the night. I tucked my hands inside my jacket and scrunched my shoulders as the distance between us grew and grew.

My birthday celebration continued that night as we hopped from one bar to another. But my heart, needless to say, clearly wasn't into it. Literally. I'd left it back at the restaurant. So when the festivities ended, I said my thanks and headed with haste back to the restaurant. Fuck if I wasn't too late. The place was sealed up tight. No Glenn in sight. I shut my eyes and pictured our brief tryst, my smile momentarily returning. "I'll be back, Glenn," I whispered. "Count on it."

And back I came, waiting a few days so as not to seem as

desperate as I really was. And, man, was I ever desperate. That kiss, those eyes, both were impossible to forget. Not that I wanted to.

The place was jammed, just like my birthday night. I sat at a lonely table for one and waited. And waited some more. Barely nibbling on my cold spring roll. No Glenn. And when the waiter came to fill up my tea, I finally managed to ask, "Um, is Glenn working tonight?"

He smiled. "Sorry," he said. "Glenn doesn't work here anymore. Yesterday was his last night."

Too late. Too fucking late. Murphy's law was having a field day with my life. "Oh, okay, um, do you know where he went? I mean, um, to work?"

The guy shrugged. "Beats me. Big town. Lots of restaurants." He turned and walked away.

Big town, he said. Lots of restaurants. Not good, not good at all. I groaned and downed the remnants of my meal before heading out. Lots of restaurants. All listed online, of course. Cheaper to call than to eat at every one, I figured.

Here's how my search went down: I phoned at least twenty restaurants a night, all from the library stacks, off in a deserted corner just after classes. As if graduate school wasn't exhausting enough. Still, what choice did I have? Oh, yeah, yeah, the obvious choice would've been to throw in the towel, to move on, to find another Mr. Right Now. But I liked the towel. I hoped to wrap it around his narrow waist some day as we exited the shower together. Call me a hopeless romantic. Nah, nix that; call me a hopeful romantic. I made it through a quarter of the listings in just a few days. Not that I found Glenn. But I would, and soon. I just knew I would. I had to.

But soon didn't come soon enough. Or at all, for that matter.

I finished dialing the restaurants whose names started with *R, S, T, U,* and *V,* and I knew that few remained from *W, X, Y,* and *Z.* I was fucked. And not in a good way. He was gone. For good. Well, not for good. For bad. Really bad. What was I to do? Walk the streets staring at every guy who passed, hoping beyond hope that one of them would be him? Expand my search to nearby towns? I closed my laptop, flicked off my cell, and dropped my head onto the cubicle desk. "Damn," I cursed. "Where the *fuck* are you, Glenn?"

And then, from out of the silence, "Hello?" A voice floated from somewhere. "Did someone just say my name?"

Was Murphy's law playing tricks on me again? I poked my head around the side of the cubicle and looked down the hall, and there he was, striding toward me, his eyes shining like beacons. "Glenn?" I managed, standing up, my knees wobbling at the unexpected shock of seeing him again, and so out of place.

"Jeff? That you?" he asked, his pace quickening.

"What are you doing here?" we both asked at the same time.

"I go to school here," we both said, again simultaneously, smiles stretching wide across our faces.

"Wait," I said, "My turn." I paused, collecting myself as best I could. "But I thought you were a waiter."

"No," he replied, with a chuckle. "I'm a poor grad student who sometimes needs to work in order to make ends meet."

Which explained why I couldn't find him, despite my best efforts. "Ah," I ah-ed. I hesitated, looked down, then back up, drowning in his magnificent pools of blue. "I, um, went back to the restaurant. You, um, you weren't there."

The chuckle grew to a hearty laugh. "Yeah, well, my ends met. For the time being." He paused, his hand reaching out to hold mine, his fingers entwining with my fingers. "You, uh, you went back to the restaurant to, to find me?"

I squeezed his hand. "I hate sushi," I told him.

"So why go back?"

My heart pulsed. *Boom. Boom. Boom.* "Well, *you* I like."

He closed the gap between us, holding me tight—at long last—in his strong arms. His lips brushed mine, and he rested his hands on the small of my back, just under my shirt, and he whispered, "Did you get that wish you asked for?"

I nodded. "In spades, now," I replied, my mouth full on his, a kiss to be forever remembered. Perfect.

Then something long and thick and hard poked me. "Chopsticks?" I asked.

He pulled away, just an inch, locking eyes with me as he led my hand to his crotch. "Not this time," he replied. "It's another birthday present. Belated. Want to unwrap it?"

"Fuck yeah," I rasped, the zipper sliding down as I again melted into him, my hand on the best present ever.

And once the package is opened, there's no taking it back. Not that I would ever want to. Sometimes birthday wishes really do come true.

THE FALLS

Natty Soltesz

Randy Perletti came out of the closet when he was nineteen. His mom cried. His dad stayed silent and retreated to the backyard shed. A few hours later his older sister, Becky, called from her apartment in Pittsburgh.

"How could you do this to them?" she said with all the righteousness she could muster from her three-and-a-half years as a psychology major. "You're their only son, Randy. Can't you understand how this would affect them? Don't you want to get married and have kids someday?"

Randy sighed. For much of his first semester at college he'd been holed up in his dorm room exchanging blow jobs with his well-hung roommate, Chuck. Chuck had undergone a Christian reawakening just a week before, though, and had asked for a room exchange.

Randy was no stranger to curious straight boys and their post–blow job blues. Usually he'd ignore the pain, but this one had left him feeling weirdly courageous. If God took stock in the fact that you liked the smell of your lacrosse-playing roommate's sweaty balls, well, what did that say about God?

"Love is the most sacred thing you can experience," Becky continued, "and you want to write it off, just like that."

"Give me a fucking break, Becky. Just 'cause you have a boyfriend now after, like, eight years of crying into your pillow and listening to Karen Carpenter doesn't make you an expert on relationships." Becky didn't say anything. "I'm gay. Get the fuck over it." He hung up the phone and headed upstairs.

"Where are you going?" his dad called from the couch.

"To my room," Randy said, exasperated. His parents watched him, as though fascinated that gay people ascended staircases to rooms.

Fortunately his parents were still in shock that spring when Randy dropped his second bomb and told them he wasn't going back to school. They even let him move back home. He got a job washing dishes at the diner and another job cleaning buildings on Market Street. He was saving money (he wasn't sure what for) and still had enough for gas and a weekly lid of pot. He was happy at home in Groom, Pennsylvania, where things were safe and familiar. Most of his high school buddies were still around. A few of them were more than pleased to have him back, for Randy was as discreet as he was up for anything.

Randy met Becky's boyfriend, Dominic Posvar, for the first time on Memorial Day at his parents' house.

"I've heard a lot about you," Randy said, shaking Dom's hand which, like the rest of him, was thick and strong.

"Me, too," Dom said, and he blushed. Becky was engaged to Dom by then and was in the midst of planning an insanely elaborate ceremony, wringing as much stress and drama from the process as she could. Randy figured it was her punishment to the world for not having noticed her sooner.

Randy was asked to be a groomsman, but stuck to the sidelines as the wedding date neared, grateful that the family's attention had been diverted from him. Dom seemed glad to acquiesce to Becky's whims and go with the flow. He wasn't unfriendly to Randy, nor did he reach out, but as the weeks went by Randy started noticing things: glances that lasted too long, nervous tics whenever they were together in a room. A telepathic dialogue was manifesting itself.

Dom bunked at the Perletti house the night before the wedding, while Becky stayed with her bridesmaids across town. Randy was up late watching TV when Dom came downstairs, wearing a white V-neck T-shirt that hugged his muscles, and blue pajama pants.

"Hey," he said to Randy. Randy hadn't expected anyone to be up this late and was wearing just his boxers. He didn't mind showing off his thin, defined body, which was tanned a golden brown.

Dom seemed half asleep. He rubbed his hands over his close-shorn, sandy-haired head, then shuffled to the kitchen and poured a glass of milk. He sat down on the couch next to Randy.

"What are you doing up?" Randy asked.

"Just jittery I guess. What about you?"

"Too much coffee at the rehearsal dinner. Well, that and I'm nervous too. First family gathering since...well...you know." Dom's head snapped to the TV. He took a too-quick drink of his milk and it spilled down the sides of his mouth.

"Crap," he said and lifted his shirt to wipe his face. Randy couldn't help but look. Dom's stomach was thick but tight, with a blondish happy trail that disappeared into his pajama pants.

"I guess it's normal to be nervous," Randy said, shifting his gaze. "Anyway I'm sure Becky would understand if you changed your mind." Dom smiled. He took another swig from the glass, this one more successful.

"I just wish it was over," Dom said. Randy gave him a sympathetic smile. After a moment, Dom lifted his shirt again. He wiped his mouth even though there wasn't anything there, and he did it slowly. He watched Randy gaze at his body as he tugged his shirt back down, until their eyes met and they realized they'd caught each other in the act.

So Becky got hitched and Randy got drunk. The new couple bought a house in Groom just a few blocks from the Perletti house. Dom, who had a bachelor's degree in communications, took a job managing the Groom Motor Lodge on the highway while Becky looked for work.

One night after the newlyweds came for dinner at the Perletti house, Randy fell asleep in the easy chair while Dom watched TV from the couch. The first thing Randy noticed when he awoke was Dom watching him. Dom quickly averted his eyes back to the TV, his face flushing. Randy reddened himself when he realized what Dom had been staring at—a conspicuous tent in his sweats from the industrial-sized boner he'd sprung in his sleep.

The next Friday Becky recruited her brother to help paint the new couple's bedroom. When he arrived Dom was already rolling paint onto the walls, and Becky was getting dressed for a job interview in Latrobe.

"They called me at the last minute," she said. "Hopefully you guys will be all right?"

"I'm sure we can manage," Randy said. Becky looked to her husband.

"Dom? You'll be okay with just Randy here?"

"Why wouldn't we be?" Randy said again. Becky ignored him.

"Sure, honey," Dom said, and Becky said she'd be back in a few hours.

There was some brief awkwardness after she left, but small talk was one of Randy's strengths, and he easily maneuvered them into friendly waters.

"Is married life all it's cracked up to be?" he asked as he loaded up his brush with periwinkle paint.

"I wasn't expecting anything, I don't think," Dom said. "It's nice though. You know—comfortable. I don't have to wonder about, like, going out on a Friday night, looking for whatever, getting drunk. That gets old."

"You don't like to drink?" Randy said.

"Well, sometimes I do."

"Good, cause I brought a six-pack. We can split it." By the time they finished painting they had two beers left. They were cleaning off their brushes and rollers in the utility room, the close quarters heady with the smell of sweaty bodies.

"Wish the pool was still open," Dom said.

"We should go up to Bolivar Falls," Randy said. "You ever been?"

"No," Dom said, then hesitated. Into the vacuum of his silence rushed sexual tension. Randy hadn't intended it, but there it was.

"I've heard of it," Dom continued, whacking a brush off the side of the sink. "We could take the rest of the beer."

"Sure," Randy said, his heart picking up speed. "Becky won't care, right? We can leave her a note or something."

"Don't bother," Dom said.

After a ten-minute drive they started the two-mile hike into the woods. They were soaked in sweat again by the time they got to the falls, a forest glen with a creek that dropped off into a deep pool. There was graffiti on the rocks and some strewn-about trash, but it had a secretive charm.

"I guess we can go in in our underwear?" Randy said.

"Sure," Dom said, emboldened by the beer and the beauty of the place. He stripped down and Randy followed suit. Dom's tighty-whities hugged the generous curves of his muscular butt and acted like a sling for his beefy cock. Randy was embarrassed to reveal his patterned bikini briefs—a purchase he'd made out of boredom and horniness one night while stuck at the mall with his mom.

Dom swept his eyes up and down Randy's body and Randy did the same to Dom. Before either could register anything Dom turned and ran for the ledge, springing himself over the waterfall and into the air, crashing into the pool below.

"It's freezing!" he called. Randy approached the edge. He felt the slick rock beneath his feet. He jumped, fear and release rushing through his body for a drawn-out instant before he plunged into the water.

"It feels fucking amazing!" Randy said, his breathing short and shallow. They laughed with exhilaration.

Later they lay on the warm rock above the waterfall.

"Did you have a good time at the wedding?" Dom asked.

"Yeah, man."

"It wasn't awkward for you? I mean, you said you thought it might be."

"Well, the open bar helped." Dom laughed. "I don't care what people think of me, anyway," Randy said. Dom drank the last of his beer.

"You mean the fact that you're..."

"Gay. Yeah. That."

"Yeah," Dom said. Birds squawked in the trees. "I was wondering... Like, how did you know you were? I mean, did you ever date girls?"

"Yeah I dated girls. I even had sex with a few of them."

"Really?"

"Yeah. But I always did stuff with my friends, too. And eventually I realized that stuff was more interesting."

"You messed around with your friends?" Dom said.

"Yeah."

"Like what kind of stuff?"

"Like, you know. Kissing. More than kissing," Randy said. Dom brought the beer bottle to his lips, tipped it back even though it was empty. Randy took a deep breath. "Did you ever do stuff like that? Like before you met Becky?"

"No," Dom said. He turned his head to Randy and smiled. "Not even kissing."

"Kissing's easy," Randy said. "You know—noncommittal."

Dom laughed. "I'd try that. Kissing a guy."

"It's not much different from kissing a girl," Randy said, nervously plugging his thumb into the mouth of his beer bottle.

Dom stood up. He tossed his empty bottle into the weeds and turned toward Randy. His half-hard cock tented his transparent briefs. Randy set down his bottle and stood up next to him, his hefty dick also visibly at half-mast.

"You want to?" Dom said.

"Kiss?" Randy said.

"Yeah," Dom said. They moved toward each other, their cocks hardening. When they came together an involuntary, almost reflexive force took over. Their mouths locked and their tongues dueled, desire passing between them thick and hot as molten rock. Randy moved his hands to Dom's back. Dom placed his hands on the smooth sides of Randy's torso. Making out with Dom felt natural and breathtaking, but it was just too much. Randy had to break away.

"Thanks," Dom said, looking at the ground, and the word

was a hollow thud. They dressed and headed to the car. The world, having disappeared for a moment, rushed back like a tsunami. They rode home in silence, each mile getting them closer to the lives they'd upended.

The strange thing was that after that day, hard as they tried to avoid each other, Becky seemed to do all she could to bring them together. She went whole hog in enlisting Randy's help with their house, making dates that Randy always managed to blow off.

"I saw they just opened a record store on Market Street," she said one night over dinner at the Perlettis'. "You and Dom both like music—you guys should go down there together!"

"Sure," Randy said, and Dom nodded politely, while Becky eyed them like they were lab rats.

"Do you like Dom?" Becky asked her brother one night after dinner. Randy was washing dishes while Becky sat at the kitchen table. Dom had already gone home.

"Of course," Randy said. "Dom's a good guy."

"I think he's about the best-looking guy I've ever seen," Becky said. "Don't you think he's good looking?"

"Yeah, he is," Randy said. "He's got a handsome face."

"Are you happy for me?"

"Of course I am. I'm happy for all of us, 'cause if you hadn't gotten laid soon you would've drove us all nuts."

"Hush up," Becky said. "I hate it when you talk like that." She dipped her finger into a candle, coating the tip with hot wax. "I never thought a guy like Dom would *look* at me, let alone *marry* me."

"Don't say that," Randy said.

Becky shrugged. "I know I'm not the cutest button in the box. But there was Dom, sitting across from me in my Shakespeare class, and he just…I don't know…*listened* to me. Made me feel like I was worth his time. I asked him to go out, and he did. I'd never asked a guy out before. Can you believe that?" Randy toweled off a plate and stacked it with a clink.

"I can," he said, turning toward his sister. "You don't give yourself enough credit, Becky. You've always been shy, but you're great. People just don't get to see it." Becky smiled and cast her eyes downward. Randy went to bed that night with a heavy heart.

On Labor Day Becky arranged a picnic at their parents' house. Dom wore a pair of thin khaki shorts that made his ass look like wrapped cantaloupes. In the chaos of aunts and uncles and cousins Randy lost track of his brother-in-law. He had to piss, so he entered the quiet house and went up the stairs to the bathroom. The door was closed and the shower was running. He figured it was his dad, so he walked in and shut the door behind him.

"I gotta pee," he said after he'd already unzipped. He heard the shower turn off. "Just gimme one second." The curtain pulled back and Randy turned his head. There was Dom, naked, wet, and already half-hard.

"Shit," Randy said. "Sorry." Dom, who'd needed to clean up after knocking whiffleballs around with the kids in the ninety-degree heat, locked eyes with Randy. He didn't move a muscle except for his cock, which lurched like a thing from the dead until it was standing straight up.

Randy could've left the room. It was probably the right thing to do. But instead he stepped forward and wrapped his hand around Dom's fat cock. He raised his face to meet Dom's mouth. As they made out their hands moved like wildfire, Dom ripping off Randy's clothes, Randy feeling every inch of Dom's body. Randy knelt down, his shorts around his thighs and his hard cock jutting out. He took Dom's cock in his mouth.

Dom's lungs deflated. A few passes of Randy's mouth and

throat around his cock and Dom was almost juicing. Randy licked his way up his brother-in-law's body, munched on his pecs and nipples, then trailed his tongue down Dom's thigh. He flipped him around. Dom braced himself against the shower wall. Dom's ass was a gift, big and perfect, and Randy dove in. His pink, deep asshole seemed to invite Randy to dig deeper with his tongue. Dom whimpered and pushed back harder.

Randy stood and dropped his shorts so that his buckle clanged against the floor. He grabbed a bottle of shampoo and lubed himself up. He pressed his cock to Dom's asshole and in moments he slid inside. Dom stifled a cry but didn't protest as Randy porked him balls-deep. A minute or so of thrusting and Randy was blasting inside Dom's virgin butt and Dom was spraying the shower wall.

They didn't talk as Randy slid out, pulled on his pants, and left. He went to his bedroom and locked the door, caught his breath. When he came back out Dom was with the rest of the family on the patio, freshly showered and freshly fucked. He had a noticeable glow, and even nodded to acknowledge Randy's entrance.

"It was like you tripped a switch in me," Dom would say years later about that afternoon. "I instantly knew how sex was supposed to feel. I felt so relieved." Randy had apparently fucked the fear right out of Dom, and Dom got bold. Two days later he came knocking on Randy's bedroom door. Randy tossed his liquid-crinkled issue of *Mandate* on the floor, zipped up, and answered the door.

"What are you doing here?" Randy said, ushering a wild-eyed Dom inside.

"I told Becky I was borrowing a record," he whispered. Dom impulsively leaned forward and kissed him, knocking their mouths together so hard it hurt. "Here," he said, and handed Randy a key. The plastic, diamond-shaped key ring had the number 428 imprinted on both sides. "I got this room for tonight."

"For us?" Randy said.

"You don't want to come," Dom said, his face falling.

"No, no, of course I do, it's just...Jesus. Okay. When?"

"After two. I'm supposed to be doing paperwork in the back office but the night clerk won't notice." Randy took the key. Dom made it halfway down the hall before Randy thought to call him back. He grabbed the first record off his stack and shoved it in Dom's hands. Dom looked at it: Abba, *Arrival*.

"I already have this one," he said.

Sex at the hotel that night was less furtive than before but even more frenzied. Randy dropped three loads into his brother-in-law in less than two hours—one down his gullet and two in his increasingly insatiable butt.

"I love your dick in me," Dom admitted as they lay beside each other watching the blank TV, the Zen-like hum of the motel room thrumming through them. Then, "Becky wants a baby."

"I'm supposed to be saving money to move to the city," Randy said.

"You're moving?"

"That was the plan. I don't know what the fuck I'm going to do now."

"Me neither," Dom said. They fucked again.

For two more weeks they met at the motel, until Randy couldn't take it anymore and put all he'd saved on a security deposit for an apartment in Pittsburgh. He moved in the middle of the night, telling no one until he called his parents the next day.

That October, Randy heard from his mom that Dom was leaving his sister. No particulars were offered. Randy sensed his mom knew—or at least suspected—more than she was letting on, but he didn't press the issue.

He lay low all winter. He hadn't spoken to Dom since he'd left, though on several occasions he'd driven all the way back to Groom just to see if Dom's car was still parked outside the motel, which it always was.

That spring Randy came home to visit. The divorce had gone through. Becky was even dating a guy named Hugo that she worked with at the state mental hospital in Torrance.

"He likes bird-watching," Randy's mother reported. Randy was weeding her garden. "That's what they do together in their free time, watch birds."

"He sounds nice," Randy said. He'd tried to call his sister the week previous and she'd hung up on him.

"Your Aunt Mary called. She wants the whole family up for the Fourth of July. A reunion, she says. It's a ridiculous idea but you know how she gets."

"Hmm," Randy said, yanking plants.

"Did I ever tell you that your father used to date your Aunt Mary when they were in high school?"

"Huh? No," Randy said.

"They were in love—so *she* said. I suppose she must have felt they were—"

"Her and Dad? How long did they date?"

"Oh, a few years, I think. Even after high school. In fact they talked about getting married at one point."

"You're kidding," Randy said, sitting up to look at his mother, who was gazing into the distance.

"Even today I catch her looking at him. Maybe I just think I do. Who knows?" She shrugged. "Love is love and it doesn't care about anything but itself."

With that she walked away, leaving Randy with a head full of questions and his knees in the dirt.

SQUEAMISH

Simon Sheppard

'm trying to imagine his life. I'm trying to imagine their lives
together. Life together, singular. Master and slave.

From the outside, ordinary. Ordinary house in middle-class
suburbia, an unremarkable Japanese car in the drive. Jay gets
out of the car. Midthirties, not bad looking. One of the millions
who spend their days at a keyboard, staring at pixels. He walks
into the house, bags of groceries in his arms.

Jay locks the door behind himself. Puts the groceries away.
Strips naked. Naked except for a thin silver chain and tiny
padlock around his throat. He gets on his knees and awaits the
arrival of his master. Who will command him, use him, beat him
if he fails to please.

I'm trying my best to imagine this life.

"Nonjudgmental" is reckoned a very good thing to be. And
I'm as hip as the next guy to the reputed pleasures of a little
spanking, a few ropes. So when I think of him acting as though
he's been stripped of his will, playing the part of a robot with

a dick, I get pissed off that it makes me a bit queasy. Because anything goes between consenting adults, right? And who am I to judge?

His former lover, that's who I am. The guy who lived with Jay for twenty-three months and five days. Who knew his naked body like the contours of my own. Who wanted nothing but the best for him. Who still wants to think well of him, whatever he's up to, whatever he's become. So is it jealousy, then, that I feel when I think of him sleeping on the floor, chained to the foot of Rik's bed? Or concern for him, for his well-being? Or maybe it's both, and something else as well, something it's just not cool to talk about. Moral disapproval.

We were on Maui, our two weeks at the beach, when I first got wind of what was to come. It was our last day, we were walking hand in hand in the sunset.

"Brett, I need something more from this relationship." We'd been talking about something else, something neutral, the flight back, I don't know. So this threw me for a loop.

"Something more?"

"More, bigger, deeper. Bigger."

"Like?" I'm thinking, *Don't do this, not on our last night here, this perfect sunset, leave it alone.*

"You don't ask enough of me, demand enough out of me."

"Jay, honey, you're an adult. You feel like you need to give me more, then give me more. But I'm happy the way things are."

"You are? Yeah, you are." He squinted into the setting sun. The waves were crashing, I suddenly noticed. There was something odd in his voice. "That's the problem, see? You're satisfied, I'm not."

Please don't do this. Wait till we're back on the mainland.

"Yeah, Jay, you're right. I'm satisfied. Not always, sure, but usually. I like you. Love you. Love what we have together. What do you need, Jay? What do you think you need?"

"I need to be owned. I want you to own me."

"Oh, for god's sake…"

After dinner we went back to the room. The sex we had was perfunctory, ending in more-or-less defeat. I curled up into a fetal ball, my back to Jay. I felt uneasy, sure that I'd failed him, failed some test I hadn't even known I'd been taking.

Jay, I'm remembering you there, that next morning as we dressed for the flight. The downy blond hair on your newly tanned chest, on your forearms, shining gold in the morning sun. I suppose he's shaved your body now. I suppose you're happy now. I don't know what your life is now. I don't even know whether I want to know. Or whether I want to know if you ever think of me.

Back in Sacramento, we didn't talk about it for a while. It seemed best to patch things up, paper things over, go on with the little life we'd constructed for ourselves. When we had sex I tried to be more dominant. Pinned Jay's arms down when I fucked him. Spat in his mouth, stuff like that. We'd role-play a little. He'd call me "Sir," which felt strange at first, but grew to feel more natural as time went by. "I'm yours, Sir. Do what you want. My body is yours to use." I mean, what guy wouldn't want to hear that? But sometimes, just before the crucial moment, I'd get this thought, this very straight-male thought: *Am I man enough for this bitch?* Which didn't do wonders for my latex-clad erection.

And he'd bring home magazines, *Drummer* and *Powerplay*, and others that he wouldn't let me share. Magazines I found hidden in his dresser drawer like the *Penthouse* collection of some pimply teenage boy. *Bound and Gagged. Urban Slave.* I

never let on that I found them. Even a boyfriend's entitled to a
secret life, right?

Secrets. His secrets, which now belong to someone else.
Lock, stock and barrel. Body and soul.

Fuck, why am I writing all this, flaying myself in public?
Easy answer: because I can't say this to him. Not allowed.
Right, "not allowed." Master Rik won't let me talk to my ex-
lover. Technically, Rik won't let Jay listen to me. Same thing in
practice. I'll get to that.

So we're back in Sacramento, and when Jay was out of
the house one day, at the gym or somewhere, I tried to get a
handle on this stuff. I went into his dresser drawer and guiltily
pulled out the pile of *Urban Slaves*. There were these articles:
"Training the Novice Bitchboy," "The Art of Contractual Servi-
tude," stuff like that. And photos of guys. Guys wearing leather
dog collars, tied up, cowering at the jackbooted feet of their
respective masters.

I flipped to the classified ads, which made up the bulk of
each issue. *WM cigar-smoking master, total top, will interview
applicants, 25-35, fit, any race, for live-in position of total
submission. B&D, S&M, WS. Novices considered. Reply to
Box 74666, and be quick about it, pig-boy.* The ad was circled.
Jay had circled the ad. And other ads, ads like it, were circled as
well. Several in each issue.

Jealousy roared through the pit of my stomach, unexpectedly
intense, disappointingly conventional. Premonitions of disaster.
And just the hint of a lustful tremor in my crotch. Because I've
been around enough so that this kind of thing is not exactly new
to me, not repulsive or shocking. It's even, let's face it, more
than a little sexy.

As I was unzipping my fly, I heard Jay's key click into the
front door. I stuffed the magazines back in the drawer and

resolved to try being nastier to him in the sack. Though I drew the line at smoking cigars.

I'm sorry, the tone of this is wrong. Too flippant, too in-control. Jay, you broke my heart. You broke my fucking heart. I cried for you, Jay. I bet your master doesn't cry.

You busted my life to bits, and now I'm making a jokey little story out of it, to cushion me from the pain, the gut-gnawing frustration. Though I must confess that part of me still thinks that the idea of the middle-aged, slightly chubby computer jockey I knew and loved, the idea of you, Jay, crawling on all fours and pretending to be a Labrador retriever is, well, silly.

You are, aren't you? Maybe right now. Crawling on your hands and knees, panting, whimpering, licking his outstretched palm. Eating from a dog dish on the floor. Awaiting his commands. Oh, fuck, oh, fuckfuckfuck.

It's such an old story, if you strip it of its whips and chains. As old as time, as familiar as everything you see on TV. If you strip it of its whips and chains.

When September came, Jay headed to San Francisco for a weekend of opera. It's a passion of his I never could relate to...all those overwrought emotions in languages that I don't understand. So he went off alone, calling in sick on Friday. Three performances: Wagner, Verdi, someone else. Friday night, Saturday night, Sunday matinee. And when Jay got back he was different, changed in a way I couldn't put my finger on. I assumed he'd had sex with someone else. It had happened before, how many times I don't know, but we'd always agreed that that was kind of okay. We always had an open relationship, more or less. But this time the awkwardness, the distance between us seemed unbridgeable, as though we'd never again relax into the comfortable life of the day-to-day. There's a line from a Leonard Cohen song: "And when you came back, you were nobody's wife." Something like that. It was something like that.

"What's happened?"

"What do you mean, what's happened?"

"You're different. You've changed. What happened in San Francisco?"

"I don't want to talk about it."

As we approached our second anniversary, the sex became infrequent. One night I tried to liven things up with a bit of spanking. I discovered that I liked the feeling of my hand coming down on Jay's butt. At first Jay seemed interested, then bored. His dick collapsed.

That was that.

In November, Jay was off for another weekend in San Francisco. Puccini. Mussorgsky. When he came back there were bruises all over his back and butt. Purplish. Yellowish. He wouldn't talk about it. It made me sad for him. And it made me jealous. *There are places he is going where I cannot or will not follow,* I thought. *Or, more to the point, lead him.*

That month there was lots of early snow. We went cross-country skiing at Tahoe. We'd both worked up a sweat and were way out in the silent, snowy woods when he told me.

"I'm leaving you."

He always does this when we're on vacation.

"Oh, yeah?" What's somebody supposed to say?

"Next month, before Christmas. I'm moving to San Francisco. I've already handed in my resignation at the office."

"You what?" *This isn't happening. There's some mistake. There's some way back from this.*

But the way back led through a sudden snowstorm, wind whipping cold in our faces. And a steep downhill where I lost control, fell, twisted my ankle and ended up stupid and helpless, lying in the snow.

That's when you told me about your master, Jay, on the drive back. You kept your eyes on the road as you drove.

"I've signed a full-time slavery contract with a guy in San Francisco. A *man* in San Francisco." Like I'm just a "guy" but he, this unknown, hairy, dominant beast, he's a Real Man. Because he wants to order you around. Because he wants to own your flesh, will even sign a paper to that effect. It made me think of heterosexuals, a man and his wholly owned wife. A queer marriage that even Jesse Helms could love. I've heard that most leathermen are Republicans. I'm beginning to understand this.

And you shoved a CD in the player. Callas. Maria Callas shrieking sorrow as we sped through the mountains. Ari left Callas for Jackie; a has-been soprano just couldn't compete with the World's Greatest Widow. And now this, you leaving me for Master Whoever. It's the kind of thought a gay man—okay, a queen—would have. Opera and soap opera. Your new master wouldn't think in those terms. He'd think like a real man, like those dominant guys in the back pages of *Urban Slave*. He'd be thinking of Attila the Hun. Or football. My ankle ached.

When we got home you unpacked the car while I limped into the house. And that was that. I didn't argue. Maybe I felt that argument was futile. Maybe I wanted to maintain my dignity. Maybe I should have fought harder for you. And maybe that wouldn't have mattered at all.

* * *

It didn't take Jay long to move out. He left one day when I was at work—to avoid a scene. I'd known it was coming, but it was still a shock when I got home and discovered that he was irreversibly gone. As though I'd walked into the wrong house. As though I were living someone else's life. I couldn't even cry. I got drunk instead.

I decided against looking for a roommate. It seemed better to live with the purity of Jay's absence. A void unsullied by the presence of another man, some unknown homosexual who'd leave his hair bunched up in the shower's drain.

Day after day, I went to work. I came home to an empty house. I got angry. I threw Jay's things across the room, the few things he'd left me. I had a drink. A second one. I went to bed. I lay in bed alone. And finally went to sleep. Day after day. Night after night.

The question I keep returning to is "Why?" Why I let it all happen so easily, why I didn't fight and argue, struggle to keep you from the clutches of your master. I suppose pride had a lot to do with it; having already been told in so many words that I wasn't man enough for you, I'd be damned if I'd get down on my knees and whimper and beg.

And what, after all, could I have said to change your mind? That I wanted to be your Master, your Owner, your Absolute God? Neither of us would have believed that. As I stood there watching you empty out your dresser drawers, you told me you'd found your master through an ad you'd placed in *Urban Slave*. "Want to see it?" you asked, all innocence, salt in the wound.

Semi-novice, 34, 5' 10", 180, seeks true master who will train, dominate, and use me. I need to serve without limits, to become the property you wish me to be. Humiliation, subjugation, pain. Willing to relocate. Respond Box 32843. Thank you, Sir!

How could you have placed that ad, Jay? What choice did I have but to lose you? How could I compete with the fascist of your dreams?

Weeks went by. No word from Jay. Before he left, he'd told me that the slavery contract—slavery contract!—allowed for communication between him and me. But the promised phone call never came. Just, at last, a postcard with a single sentence: *I've been forbidden further contact with you.*

I kept thinking of a photo I'd seen in *Urban Slave*: a naked man is shackled spread-eagle to a stone wall, a ball gag in his mouth. His genitals are tied up, distorted. There is terror, real or feigned, in his eyes. When I thought of this man (which I did, often), he had Jay's face. Sometimes I had to jack off before my mind was able to move on to something else.

Weeks passed, and then I was awakened by a phone call in the middle of the night. It was Jay, sounding desperate, speaking in a whisper. "I'm really frightened, Brett."

"What is it?"

"Can't talk now. He might hear." And then he gave me, twice, a phone number and address.

"Tomorrow's a work day," I said. "But I'll be there Saturday. I'll get there as soon as I can."

Jay started to say something, but the phone went dead. When I rang back, there was just a busy signal.

It was the phone call I'd both prayed for and feared. The next day at work I could hardly concentrate. By noon I gave up. I told the boss I was sick, and hurried home to change for the drive. I was on my way to rescue Jay, though how I'd do that, I had no idea.

When I got to our—to *my*—place, there was a message on the answering machine. Jay. His voice was flat and toneless. He was in perfect control.

"I was wrong, I was being foolish. I'm perfectly all right. Stay there, don't come to San Francisco. I've found what I was looking for. Please don't fuck it up. And please tear up that phone number and address. This is the last you'll ever hear from me. I'm sorry if I scared you. I'm okay."

Two very different thoughts tortured me: *He needs me* and *He doesn't need me at all.* I got in the car and drove toward the suburbs of San Francisco. Halfway there I had to take a piss, but rather than stopping, I held it in. The mounting discomfort lent a sense of urgency, provided a certain strange pleasure.

I got there. Parked in the driveway next to a blue Toyota. Jay's car. I was unsure who'd answer my knock. The door opened. It wasn't the unknown Master Rik, as I'd expected and half-feared. It was Jay, wearing only a studded dog collar and a little leather pouch that just barely contained his dick.

"You've made the drive for nothing." He sounded urgent, angry. "I told you not to come. I can never see you again."

From inside the house, an unremarkable voice. "Tell him to go away, boy. *Now.*"

Jay turned away from me. His back was crosshatched by nasty purplish welts and bruises. Traces of crusted blood.

"Your back!"

He looked back over his shoulder. "I've been disciplined for making contact with you. If you don't want me to be punished even more, you'll go. Now." I looked into his gray eyes. There was nothing there, nothing I could read.

The door closed. I got back in my car. I thought about driving straight back to Sacramento without taking a piss, holding it in until I lost control, until my jeans were soaked through and piss ran down my leg. Instead, I stopped at a nearby Burger King, used the restroom, and bought myself a Whopper.

That's the last I heard from Jay. Letters I sent him came back unopened. Phone calls I made always reached an answering machine, and never got returned.

I tried to talk myself through my obsession. It's like any other triangle, I told myself, if you ignore the welts and bruises. A man's wife leaves him for a diesel dyke. A poor guy's boyfriend leaves him for a millionaire. Someone just doesn't have what another person wants, what it takes. It's simple. If you ignore the welts and bruises.

My friends, those whom I could tell about this, got sick of hearing the story. They were right; there was really nothing more to be said. I resolved, time and again, to get on with my life.

I started dating, met a really nice guy: medical technologist, good body, great smile. Decent sex. When he stayed over, I'd awake in the middle of the night, startled by the presence of a man who wasn't Jay, asleep in what had been our bed. Unable to find my way back to sleep, I'd toss until the alarm sounded, running and rerunning the story of Jay and his master. His master, who isn't me.

One day, when I was rearranging some shelves, I picked up a book, one of those insipid thrillers you were always so fond of, and an envelope fell out, a letter unsent, addressed by you to a man I never heard of. I pulled the letter out. It was several pages long. Page two was on top. It began *...means well, but Brett just isn't what I need. I wish he were. I want him to be. But he seems so unaware of the distance between us. Or, if he is aware, unwilling to change things. You don't know how hard it is to love someone and yet want to hurt him. But he's caused me so* *much pain. I need to hurt him back, and hurt him badly. It's tearing me apart. But I know that...*

I stopped reading, folded the letter back into the envelope, stamped it, and dropped it in a mailbox. Since then, I've tried my best not to think of that letter. But I wonder if it ever got to that unknown man. That man you shared your secrets with, secrets you always kept from me. God, Jay, who are you, who were you when we were together? And who the hell was I?

The months rolled by. The medical tech and I drifted apart. Neither of us very much regretted the end of our affair. I got used to an empty house. An empty bed.

I did drive to San Francisco a couple of times, to Rik's house, but when I got there, I just sat in the car. When I finally drove away again, I felt even more alone.

One day I was at an adult bookstore. I'd been hitting the video booths, to no great success. There on the magazine rack was the latest issue of *Urban Slave*. I couldn't resist. I picked it up, flipped through it. I stopped short. It was you, a picture of you. I'm sure it was, though the face was half-hidden. A photo of you all tied up. And a classified ad from, I guess, Rik, offering to loan his boy out to qualified masters. *Use My Slave,* the headline read. I felt dizzy, got a raw feeling in the back of my throat. So this was what you'd become, what you'd longed to become. A piece of meat with a gag in your mouth.

I felt sick. Sick with worry, with regret. And sick with longing, because I knew that I'd never be good enough to have you, not even on loan.

* * *

Summer came, then September. Some friends convinced me to go with them to the Folsom Street Fair, a big leather-and-Levi's event in San Francisco.

All the way there, I was scared of what I was sure I'd see: Jay, stripped to the waist, hands tied behind his back, look of adoration in his eyes, being led on a leash by a muscular, silver-haired man with a look of quiet strength. If I saw them, I had no idea of what I'd do.

When we got to the Fair, the broad expanse of Folsom Street was so crowded that I realized that Jay and I could be there all afternoon and still not run into each other. My anxiety and eagerness subsided, but only a little.

And my libido heated up. Men in leather. Men in black leather were everywhere. Could there really be so many guys into kinky sex? One of the friends I'd come with cracked that for many of these hide-clad, gym-buffed men, "S&M" meant "Stand and Model." Still, there were so many "daddies," their bare, out-of-shape butts bravely sagging from their chaps, leading their "boys" on leashes. So many men whose willing flesh had been tattooed, pierced, and, from the look of it, freshly flogged the night before. Some of this must be for real, I thought. Whatever "real" is.

On one corner, a man leaning against a brick building was getting sucked off in broad daylight. I joined a little knot of eager spectators. A well-built, shirtless black man was on his knees, blowing a lean, hairy man who was naked except for a pair of engineer's boots and a leather hood that concealed his face. The black man slid his mouth off the hard-on, which glistened in the afternoon light. The man getting blown was handcuffed to a pipe that ran along the building, above his head. The kneeling man stood, pulled his dick out, pissed on the other man, and then walked away. The hooded man, hard-on curving upward, stood alone for a moment, until a man from the crowd came forward and knelt before him, taking the black man's place.

A few years ago, all of this would have seemed utterly alien to me. Now I wasn't so sure. Had Jay found his place in a wondrous world where once-suppressed dreams are allowed to flourish in the light of day? Or was he one of a crowd of emotionally stunted men who are trapped by self-hatred, by a repression so deep that only the rituals of power and the sting of pain will allow them to accept their own desires? And what about that big, tough guy who posed on the corner of Folsom and Ninth, scowling from beneath a motorcycle cap, the one with the perfect chest? If he and I were alone, locked together in a room, what the hell would happen? What would I want to happen? Am I so different, really, from Jay and his ilk?

I was on my third or fourth beer when I thought I saw them. It looked like Jay. It looked like Jay's body, though his head was covered by a leather hood. And the man by his side, the master, the top, he could have been any ordinary-looking middle-aged man, a realtor, maybe, or a medical technologist. Somebody who wouldn't look out of place at the Opera House. Without stopping to think, I shoved my way through the crowd, over to where they were. The man in the hood looked at me. Directly at me. Gray eyes. They could have been Jay's eyes. He looked at me but didn't make a move, betray a flash of recognition. Nothing.

At that moment, for a very long beat of time, I convinced myself that it *was* Jay. And I did not want to curse him. Or rescue him from bondage. Those plans I made, sleepless at three a.m., plans to rescue him, drag him home, kiss him, rape him, those plans, I realized, don't mean shit. I'm in over my head. Maybe we all are.

And all I wanted to do, and this I still can't fully understand, was to beg his forgiveness. More than anything in the world. To get down on my knees in the middle of the street and beg him to forgive me. "I'm sorry. I'm so sorry," I wanted to say, right there, surrounded by all those men, all those forbidden, near-irresistible mutations of desire.

But the moment passed. And the two men, master and slave, moved on.

ABOUT THE AUTHORS

MICHAEL BRACKEN's short stories have appeared in *Country Boys, Ellery Queen's Mystery Magazine, Espionage Magazine, Flesh & Blood: Guilty as Sin, Freshmen, Hot Blood: Strange Bedfellows, The Mammoth Book of Best New Erotica 4, Men, Mike Shayne Mystery Magazine, Ultimate Gay Erotica 2006* and many other anthologies and periodicals.

DAVID CIMINELLO's fiction has appeared in the anthology *Portland Queer: Tales of the Rose City* and the literary journal *Lumina*. His poetry has appeared in *Poetry Northwest*, and his original screenplay, *Bruno aka The Dress Code*, was released in 2000. He lives in New York City.

L. A. FIELDS is pursuing a degree in English literature at New College of Florida. Her work has appeared in several queer anthologies, including the Bram Stoker Award–winning *Unspeakable Horror: From the Shadows of the Closet*. Her first novel, *Maladaptation*, was published in 2009 by Rebel Satori Press.

JAMIE FREEMAN lives in North Florida. He spends many late nights drinking coffee, reading old paperback mysteries, and watching black-and-white musicals on television. His short stories can be found in *Daddies, Best Gay Erotica 2010* and *College Boys*. He can be reached by email at JamieFreeman2@gmail.com.

DOUG HARRISON's (pumadoug@gmail.com) erotic ruminations have appeared in zines, twenty anthologies, and a spiritual memoir, *In Pursuit of Ecstasy*. He was active in San Francisco's leather scene, is a father and grandfather, and has a firm but gregarious leather partner with whom he experiments in Hawaii.

TREBOR HEALEY (treborhealey.com) is the author of the Ferro-Grumley and Violet Quill award–winning novel, *Through It Came Bright Colors*, as well as a collection of poems, *Sweet Son of Pan*, and a short-story collection, *A Perfect Scar & Other Stories*. He lives in Los Angeles.

DAVID HOLLY (gaywriter.org) has operated a rare book shop, worked as a hotel clerk, and lives with a cat. As for his reputed love for slinky briefs, readers meeting him would have to check for themselves. His stories have appeared in *Best Gay Erotica*, *Surfer Boys,* and *Boy Crazy*.

G. A. Li says that when she's not writing, she likes to paint—bright colors on small canvases, torn pages, odd bits pulled from the recycling bin. Her first published story, "Like They Always Been Free," appears in the science fiction anthology *Federations*, edited by John Joseph Adams, alongside stories by Anne McCaffrey and Robert Silverberg.

JAY MANDAL is from southern England. He has written three novels, *The Dandelion Clock*, *Precipice* and *All About Sex*, and three collections, *A Different Kind of Love*, *The Loss of Innocence* and *Slubberdegullion*. He is at work on another collection and some flash fiction. For excerpts visit bewrite.net/authors/jay_mandal.htm.

DAVID MAY contributed to *Drummer* and other gay skin magazines in the 1980s, published two classic story collections in the 1990s, including *Madrugada: A Cycle of Erotic Fictions*, reprinted in 2009 by Nazca Plains, and has contributed to many anthologies, including *Flesh & the Word 3* and *Best Gay Erotica 2007*. He lives in Seattle.

DAVID PUTERBAUGH's short stories have been included in *Best Gay Love Stories 2005* and *Fool for Love*. A lifelong New Yorker, David received his MFA in creative writing from Queens College, CUNY. He's online at davidpnyc.livejournal.com.

ROB ROSEN (therobrosen.com) is the author of *Sparkle: The Queerest Book You'll Ever Love* and *Divas Las Vegas*, and has contributed to more than sixty anthologies, including the Cleis Press collections *Truckers*, *Best Gay Romance* (2007, 2008, & 2009), *Hard Hats*, *Backdraft*, *Surfer Boys*, *Bears*, *Special Forces* and *College Boys*.

SIMON SHEPPARD is the author of *Hotter Than Hell and Other Stories*; *Kinkorama*; *In Deep: Erotic Stories*; and *Sex Parties 101*, and editor of the Lammy-winning *Homosex: Sixty Years of Gay Erotica*, and of *Leathermen*. His work has also appeared in more than three hundred anthologies. He lurks romantically at simonsheppard.com.

NATTY SOLTESZ (bacteriaburger.com) has had stories published in *Best Gay Erotica 2009*, *Second Person Queer* and *Best Gay Romance 2009*, regularly publishes fiction in *Freshmen*, *Mandate* and *Handjobs*, is a faithful contributor to the Nifty Erotic Stories Archive, and is writing his first novel, *Backwoods*. He lives in Pittsburgh with his lover.

JERRY L. WHEELER's fiction, erotica and essays have appeared in a number of anthologies, most recently in *I Do!*, edited by Kris Jacen, and *I Like It Like That: True Stories of Gay Male Desire*, edited by Richard Labonté and Lawrence Schimel. He is hard at work on his first novel, *The Dead Book*.

ABOUT
THE EDITOR

RICHARD LABONTÉ (tattyhill@gmail.com) lives on Bowen Island, a twenty-square-mile isle reached by ferry from Vancouver, where he edits anthologies and technical writing, reviews books, weeds a garden, walks dogs in the woods, haunts the wee local library for books to read that he doesn't have to think about, and romances Asa Liles.